SCANDALOUS
Jazmynn

Lorenza Fontenot

Copyright © 2020 Lorenza Fontenot
All rights reserved
First Edition

NEWMAN SPRINGS PUBLISHING
320 Broad Street
Red Bank, NJ 07701

First originally published by Newman Springs Publishing 2020

ISBN 978-1-64801-119-1 (Paperback)
ISBN 978-1-64801-120-7 (Digital)

Printed in the United States of America

Dedication

This book is dedicated to Randy Fontenot and Mallory Kisting.

Randy, thank you for being one of my largest supporters and for pushing me toward my dream. You always admired things I've written and pushed me to be better. I would also like to thank you for allowing me to late-night brainstorm.

Mallory, your warm heart and great soul is what made us become friends some years ago and is also what helped me write this book. You are everything! A wonderful wife, mother, daughter, and best friend.

The two of you were sent by God, and I'm so thankful for all these years we've lived life together, and I pray there's many more.

I love the both of you so much.

Chapter 1

The month of May is when my life turned upside down. Literally. May 24, 2012, to be exact. I was twenty-five going on twenty-six in the next few weeks and was still a virgin and madly in love with my best friend Devon Thomas. He didn't quite know that yet, but I was sure to tell him someday soon, at least I hoped I would build up the courage. The thought made me cringe thinking about the odds of being rejected. I will fill you in about that a little later.

I was an honors college student getting ready to graduate from the University of New Orleans, and I would be getting my PhD in counseling. I guess I'm what some would say would be a great catch. Faithful, celibate, and easy on the eyes. But I was single! I went on several dates from time to time, but there was never anyone who could capture my heart and keep it. There was John who was studying to be an industrial scientist, who by all means was fine as hell, but I found out later was unfortunately taken. I will never forget that date.

"I'm so glad you accepted this date. I've been wanting to take you out for some time now. I pass you every day between classes but you're always looking at your phone. Nice phone case, might I add. Nokia Lumina 800, do you have good service?" John asks, looking me up and down as if he could devour me, licking his lips.

I returned the gesture by very noticeably rolling my eyes. "Thanks, and yeah, it has its patchy spots, but it does pretty well." Are we going to talk about phones and phone services all night? Does he want to know who my carrier is? Or better yet, how much I pay a month?! Ugh! I look at my index finger and notice I have a chipped nail. *DAMN, CHI!* I scream to myself while scrunching up my nose, bending my lips around my teeth in a frown. I just got them done yesterday!

John, not fazed by my short response, is attempting to regain conversation. "Did it hurt?!" he said cautiously.

"What?" I look at him, puzzled. What kind of question is that? I've never heard of anyone getting hurt getting a manicure.

"Did it hurt?" he asks again.

I'm scrunching up my nose again. I don't know what I've gotten myself into, but this motherfucker is crazy! Like damn! Your mom has never gotten her nails done? Has she never taken you to the nail shop with her because she didn't have a sitter?! Like, is he just that dumb? I sarcastically ask, "Did WHAT hurt?" Because, I swear to you, if he asks about my nails, I'm fucking leaving!

John begins to grin from ear to ear, showing his well-sculpted sideburns, answering, "When you fell from heaven?"

Ugh! Well, that's not what I expected, but did he think of that all by himself? Wow. I'm not impressed! I giggle respectfully, hoping this night would go ahead and end already. I can see where this is going, and it looks like it's going to be a long night.

"So how long have you been single?" John asks.

I answer with distaste for this topic of conversation. "For a couple months." Okay, I lied. I'm not trying to act like I've just gotten out of a serious long-term relationship, but does it really matter? He doesn't know me, he's only going to know what I decide to tell him, and that's too personal to me. I feel like some guys want girls who are broken or that have been hurt so they can seem like a knight in shining armor, then they do the same thing. Rip the woman's heart to shreds. I've honestly never really been in a real relationship nor have I been hurt, but that's none of his business. I shook my head at the conversation in my mind while repeating the question back at him. "So how long have *you* been single?" I chime back.

Folding his hands while placing them on the table. "We-Well, I…" he begins as we look up to see the waiter approaching the table to take our order.

"Drinks?" asked the waiter in a high-pitched voice.

"House Cabernet Sauvignon for me please," I respond casually.

"Same here," John adds with a cocky wink.

I looked over to a couple in the far-left corner. The African American woman looked to be in her mid-twenties. She was dressed in designer Michael Kors. Everything had MK on it besides her long, strawberry blond hair. Her dress was black and turquoise with black beaded "MK" stamped all over it. It was low-cut and short with no sleeves with a sweetheart shape in the front. Shoes! OMG! They are to die for! The same print as her dress and gosh, her legs go for miles. She is a bad bitch and know it. Mmm. Mr. handsome looks a little older. Late thirties, maybe. You, sir, have to be Mediterranean… Whooooo! Dressed in that white dress shirt and dark starched down jeans and white Air Force one tennis shoes. Boy! Won't you take me home! The air force ones are out of style, though. I shook my head deep, despairingly realizing it doesn't matter. Mediterranean maybe handsome as hell, but he's not here with me.

"Jazmynn? Do you want me to order for you?"

Hmmm… Let's see. Should I? A man that knows what I want? HMM! Is it he?! Can he be trusted to order if I've excused myself to the restroom? Should I give him a try? I should. Let's see where this goes! Raising my left eyebrow with approval, "Sure." Humph! If he fucks my order up, he will eat it! I don't eat just any old thing and I sure as hell ain't eating no salad!

As he looks down nervously at the menu, I glance at the waiter. He's standing there pen in hand, waiting impatiently for John to order for me. He looked bored and completely uninterested in John's jester.

John says confidently, "Let's make two orders of that please." As he closes the menu and hands it to the waiter, he says, "I ordered the sixteen-ounce rib-eye medium rare, with a lobster tail and loaded baked potatoes. It comes with steamed vegetables and a side salad. Is that okay?"

I nodded with approval. Wow! WHAT?! That is what I was hungry for! Some good ol steak. "Melt in your mouth, not in your hand" type shit. The best way to my heart is through my belly, and bae bay, this is surely a plus to the awkward start.

The waiter nods and says, "I will be right back with your hot homemade rolls and Cabernet." John nods and returns his attention back to me. I sigh. Louder than I meant to, but quickly regain my composure by getting back to conversing.

"What do you do for fun?" I smile sweetly. Not as sweetly as I should have, but I tried. He shrugs. "Not too much, with school and my studies, I don't have much time for extracurricular activities. This is the first date I have been on in over a year." I frown. Is he serious?! It's the first date and you are telling me off the bat you won't have time for me? What an idiot! "But that doesn't mean I won't make time for you." He quickly chimes in. Mhm, way to recover!

As I bat my eyes flirtatiously, reaching my hand across the table to touch his softly, "Oh really now? So how much time do you have exactly?! I can be a little high maintenance you know. I like to be spoiled. Bathwater ran, a little takeout here and there, and oil downs at least three to four times a week…" I hold up my fingers for each number as I say them while slowly licking my lips.

He begins to blush from my obvious flirting, "Oh I can definitely make all that happen and more. My Nubian goddess, I have all the time you need! At least if you give me the chance. I would like to make you mine. ALL MINE." Wow. Just wow. It may be just me, but this dude is too corny! It's kind of weird and surely a turn-off. I quickly snatch my hand back and replace it on my lap.

As the waiter returns with our drinks and rolls, I chime back, "We'll see about that." Gave him a flirtatious wink and took a sip of wine.

He laughed a little nervously but quickly recuperates. "You're so beautiful I can stare at you all day." He reaches his left hand out for mine, and I respectfully place my left in his. He then gently pulls my left hand to his lips and kisses it. Ever so gently. It sends tingles down my spine. One touch, one kiss, that's all it took. "So what do you do for fun, Ms. Jazzi?"

I immediately yanked my hand from his grasp. Oh no, brother! That's a no-no! "Please don't call me that." I hiss, rolling my eyes. "I hate it. My mother used to call me that before she would pass out in her drunken state of coma." I say, totally disgusted. When my dad left and divorced her, she forgot she still had children to take care of. She drank her days away every chance she got, and we didn't exist unless we were giving her money for her next bottle. She's now in rehab for the fourth time. Hopefully, it helps.

He quickly apologizes, eyes wide in disbelief. "I'm sorry. I, I didn't mean to, to bring up…" Poor thing. Stuttering and everything. Bet he didn't know what hit him.

As I chuckle to myself "It's okay. You didn't know. Um, moving on, 'what do I like to do for fun?' I repeat his question, realizing I probably sounded like a crazy woman. I literally flashed out! I try to recuperate by answering saying, "Well, I love wine tasting, traveling, and writing poetry.

He takes a sip of his wine as if he's intrigued. "Oh?" he replies, raising an eyebrow. "Tell me more." He seems interested. But who knows. He's probably just trying to get me into bed like most guys I meet.

"Well, what do you want to know?" I ask.

As he goes to reply, our food is being brought to us. The steak looks scrumptious. As the food is laid out in front of us, he continues… "Well, what kind of poems do you write about?" I'm so wrapped up in the layout of the food I don't even hear him. The steak is still sizzling, the baked potatoes look so soft and creamy full of butter just the way I like them with a hint of parsley, and the lobster tail is the biggest I've ever seen!

"WHAT kind of poems do you write about, Jazmynn?" he asked with a questioning look on his face.

"Life," I reply shortly. I'm very shy when it comes to my writing and would rather be discussing the deliciousness of the food. Raising my left eyebrow and changing the subject, "So how did you know I would eat this?" I ask.

"Simple," he replied by pointing to my plate. "The best way to a woman's heart is through her stomach." he begins pointing toward his continuing with, "Although many women pretend to eat only salads," he says while laying his knife down. "The vast majority is starving for a good piece of meat and some starch!" he said with a smirk on his face. I laughed at the irony. Who knew he would know me so well? Usually, guys look at my toned physique and assume I work out and only eat trees and fruit. "True," I said. "So very true."

As we ate, we talked about school and what our plans were in life. He planned on marrying the love of his life and having a house full of kids. A big house on a hill, an outside kitchen for gatherings, and a picket fence for his dogs to run freely. He longed for that life with me. I shook my head; he has been out the game for a while. It's the first date and you're already insinuating marriage?! Hell! Who said there's even going to be a second date? All I longed for was to write a bestseller, finish college, and be successful and RICH. Oh, and let's not forget, to get laid before I grow cobwebs down there. I didn't tell him all that, though.

The waiter approached us and asked would we like any dessert. I was stuffed. The steak was immaculate and the lobster tail was almost too much to finish. But I indeed did. I don't eat many sweets, I'm watching my figure. Haha, just kidding. With the metabolism I have! Sweets wouldn't be a problem! But I declined. I love my sparkling white teeth with no cavities, and I'm more of a salty eater. John, on the other hand, ordered the NY-style cheesecake with strawberry coulis cream brulée. It looked delicious, but the toppings looked too sweet for my taste buds. When he was finally done, he paid the hostess and ushered me out the doors.

The nightlife in New Orleans is always beautiful. Everything is always lit up and you never know what you will see. To our left was a streetcar bringing people uptown. To our right was a guy dancing for tips to the song "Walk like Ronald." As silly as the song sounds, it has taken New Orleans over in the line dancing department. In front of us was a homeless woman with a sign saying "Down on my luck. Please help!" Her clothes were dirty and torn and she looked like she hadn't bathed in days or even weeks. Although her long curls were matted, she still was gorgeous and she looked so innocent and sweet. I smiled sweetly at her. It made me wonder how a person can end up in a predicament as such. John notices me staring at her and pulled out his wallet and gave her a hundred-dollar bill. Okay, big balla! I chuckled to myself. She cried in awe as she thanked him and my eyes began to swell with tears seeing his kind gesture. I wish there were more people like that in the world. Giving, loving, and appreciative. It kind of turned me on. He didn't know it, but he just may get lucky tonight! As we walked away hand in hand, I asked, "Is that something you do often?" Batting my eyes flirtatiously, squeezing his arm in hope of sculptured muscles under his evening jacket. No luck.

"Well..." He started before being cut off.

At the same time from the corner of my eye, I notice two women walking hastily up to us. The unbeWEAVEable one said... Pause. Before I can continue, I must give my definition of an "unbeweaveable" person/hairstyle. An unbeweaveable person is someone who, unbeknownst to me, chooses to wear hair extensions that neither compliments them nor looks natural. It looks like a horse's ass, but I've seen better-looking horse asses. It's unbeweaveable. It looks dry and doesn't move. In some cases can look as though something lives in it. It looks like straw sprayed with spritz or hairspray. Or twigs like a bird's nest. Some look like railroad tracks sprayed with glitter. Sometimes look like they're dipped in Kool-Aid. Green Kool-Aid. Red Kool-Aid. Purple Kool-Aid. Orange Kool-Aid. Okay, okay, that's enough. Rant over. Proceed... :)

Unbeweaveable: "John, I know betta! Motherfucker my sista at home with YOUR children wonderin' where tha fuck you at and you hoeing in da streets wit dis bitch?!"

(Oh, I forgot to mention how ghetto unbeweaveable chicks can be.) The other said, "I'm 'bout to call Makailah right na bitch an' she gon fuck you up messin wit her man!"

John, looking like a deer in headlights held both hands up in military surrender to try to stop them from coming closer, replies, "Man, y'all quit trippin this jus' my frien from school. She jus' asked me to tutor her on history. It ain't even like that. We ain't fuckin. Why y'all gotta be so messy? What y'all need to call my baby momma for?"

What the hell is going on?! Tutor me? I ask myself. Boy, please! I'm top of my class! People are beginning to stop and stare. A guy passes on side of me and does the hand signal for me to call him. He's kind of cute. A couple who were walking out of a bar is pointing and laughing hysterically, saying something about "Lets video! That girl 'bout to get her ass whipped!"

"Don' matta! You still cheating fool! What you even doin out wit' this stupid bitch?! Tutoring at a fancy restaurant. Yeah, uh-uh. You tutoring all right!" says the unbeweaveable one.

"She ain't even cute!" says the other girl rolling her eyes.

I stand there shell-shocked for a moment. What the hell is this? Is this really happening?! To me?! Oh, hell nah! "Whoa, whoa, whoa! Hold up! What the fuck? I don't know what the hell is going on, but for one, I can show you what a bitch is!" I say, pointing to the unbeweaveable one. "Bitch you don't even know me. And for two," turning to John, "Motherfucker, I thought you were single and didn't have time for extracurricular activities? What's all this?!" I move my arms around in a swirl. His face now redder than a beet. He looks like he could run away or hide in a corner. I'm trying to maintain my sanity, maturity, and lady-like poise when he replies, "Well I, I, um, didn't quite say that…" stepping back slowly."

"Do what?" I said, cocking my head to the side like a dog when it hears a weird sound while cupping my left ear. Then it hit me. My jaw drops. I realize he hadn't completely answered at dinner and my greedy ass was so caught up in the spread of the dinner I was only half listening to him. While collecting my thoughts and straightening my posture, I close my mouth point to him and say, "You know what? Never mind! I'm out! I don't have time for this bullshit!"

Both girls are grinning from ear to ear. Looking behind me and pointing at me saying "This one right here." I turn to see what they are looking at and attempt to walk away, and pow!

I see stars, and all goes black…

Chapter 2

I wake up with my head pounding and my body aching. Where the hell am I?! I look around to see machines hooked to me and a nurse and doctor talking among themselves with their backs to me.

"This is so sad! She seems like a sweet, young lady. What is this world coming to? What's wrong with this generation?!" says the nurse.

"I couldn't tell you, Maureen. She's lucky, that's for sure. I was told she was brought in by a homeless woman. The old lady could barely walk, but she carried a 130-pound woman in here with no problem. Some people just have kind hearts. I'm glad she brought her in when she did because witnesses say you could hear laughter and cheering while people just stood around while watching and filming this horrific incident. Her physical injuries are severe. She'll be here about a week. Luckily she has no broken bones, but I need to be sure there isn't any internal bleeding before I can send her home," says a tall guy in slacks and a white dress shirt.

"Where am I?!" I asked with my dry mouth in a shallow voice.

The man turns to face me and replies, "Hi, Ms. Barkley. I'm Dr. Jamison. You're at St. Patrick's hospital in New Orleans, Louisiana. Do you know why you're here and how you got here?"

"No," I reply meekly. The hell I'm doing here?

He continues with, "You were allegedly beaten by three girls."

My mind veers off. I cannot believe this shit! That's right! Those girls who came up to me and John when we walked out of the restaurant. Did he say three girls? OMG, so they jumped me?! Over a no count poor excuse of a man! Tears begin to swell in my already blurry eyes as I try to remember everything but can't. How did I get here? Did they jump me all at once, or was I already fighting one? Where did this even happen?! Think, Jazmynn! THINK!

"The police are here to get a statement," he continues, "If you're ready. If not I can ask them to come tomorrow. You may be able to remember the events, you may not, but don't be alarmed because your memory should come back fully in a day or so."

"No, it's okay. Send them in." I attempt to sit up, but wince because the pain is so intense.

Maureen comes over to assist me. She instead raises up the head of the bed and then adjusts my pillow between my back and neck. "There, there, sweetheart," she says. "Is this more comfortable?"

"Yes, ma'am," I reply meekly.

She then points to a cord with a red button on the end of it, "Press your call light if you need anything. My name is Nurse Maureen. Just ask for me." She winks and leaves out of the room with Dr. Jamison.

Two officers walked in. A Caucasian guy and a tall dark and handsome African American one. I tried to smile, but it hurt. I probably look like shit anyway. I put my hands in my lap as the questions began.

"Hi, I'm Officer Green and this is Officer Stanley. Sorry to meet you under these circumstances, but it is very important in an investigation for us to attempt to gather information as soon as possible before a victim forgets or evidence is destroyed. Do you know why you're here?" the Caucasian cop asked.

No. I'm just here just because! I shake my head. "Yes and no."

"No?" Officer Green asked.

"Yes and no," I say sarcastically.

Officer Stanley stated, "Can you tell us what happened last night? At least what you remember if you can remember anything."

I roll my already half closed eyes. What a dick! I close my eyes to replay the events of the night before. "I went out on a date to eat with John at The Court of Two Sisters on Royal Street, and…"

Officer Stanley asked, "John? Is this your boyfriend?" scribbling in a little black book.

"No, this was our first date. Anyway, we left and as we were walking out I saw this homeless lady holding a sign, saying she needed help and John gave her some money." I thought that was the sweetest thing. It brought tears to my eyes once again to know there were still generous people in the world. I wonder if she was the homeless lady who brought me in? What if he just did that trying to impress me? I quickly became angry as I began to recall the events thereafter.

"Then these two girls walked up, saying something about their sister was at home wondering where he was and he's out with me.'"

"Were you two having an affair?" asks Officer Green

I gave him the "that was the dumbest question I've ever heard" look. "No, we weren't. As I stated at the beginning, this was our first date."

"And?" asked Officer Stanley. "That's it! That's all I remember. We had a few words and I said I was out and then I turned to walk away..." I paused. My head starts to pound and the light is beginning to make my headache worse. "That's all I remember," I reply, taking a deep breath, exhaling loudly hoping they get the hint that I'm beyond annoyed.

Officer Green asked, "Did you know the females?"

"No." You freaking idiot! Sure, someone I know will jump me and put me in the hospital for going on a date with a complete stranger!

Officer Stanley said, "Do you remember what the girls looked like? We can have a sketch artist come by, or could you explain their appearance? We need as many details as possible. We plan to roll back all cameras from the nearby businesses. If we find anyone fitting any of the descriptions, and we are not positive, we will give you a call and ask that you would come into the precinct to point them out."

"I guess so." I shrug. I mean, all of us women sort of do that anyway already. Compare each other to one another. We check out if the outfit matches the shoes, purse, etc. Use a certain style we see and make it our own. And if a chick gets into it with another, best believe you will remember what they look like for the next time you see them! I come out of a trance and begin my description. "One was like five-foot-nine, but she had on heels. She wore black capris with a white wife beater. She had a short haircut and dimples. (She looked like she had gotten in a fight with a weed eater. Can I tell him that?) Oh, and she was about my color, caramel. The other was like five-foot-seven with blue jeans, looked like flip-flops and a red see-through shirt. Her hair was blue, green, and red, cut in a bob and she was a dark chocolate." As I finished my sentence I looked down at Officer Stanley's hand and noticed he had on a wedding band. Shaking my head… DAMN! Why all the cute ones always taken?

Lost in thought, mesmerized by his chiseled features wishing I was wrapped in his arms someone barges in the door screaming, "I don't give a fuck I AM family! Get the fuck out the way!" Janae! My best friend is here to see me! The officers step back as she walks past them straight to my bed hugging and kissing me on the cheeks. Grabbing me by my shoulders, making me wince at the pain she says, "Bitch! What the fuck?! I have been blasting your phone up tryna make sure you made it from your date okay. I went to the house, you weren't there, Dev hadn't talked to you, I rode around looking for you and I decided just for the hell of it to start calling hospitals 'cause you never go all night without talking to me or coming home! Hell, I thought you went meet your mama in the nut house!" She elbows me playfully in the arm with a side smile. "Just kidding, but I was so worried!" she says whirling her hands around. "I done been to the restaurant and all up and down the block questioning people!" Turning to point at the police. "These motherfuckers wouldn't tell me what happened, but I got my ways," she says proudly, grinning a sly grin. She knows so many people and can get any kind of information. She wanted to do a background check on John, but I wouldn't let her. "But anyway, I found out three hoes jumped you. You laid on the sidewalk for nearly an hour while people were filming you on their phones before some old lady pushed through the crowd and picked you up and brought you here. Man, I wish you would've called me, 'cause we sure the fuck woulda…"

Officer Stanley said, "Er, excuse me, ma'am?"

Janae, turning back to face the officers, looking like dayumm bro, said, "Yes?" She bats her eyes a little over flirtatiously.

"We were conducting an investigation interview when you barged in and we would like to finish so we can quickly apprehend the suspects."

Janae said sarcastically, "Well I would like you to handcuff me to this hospital bed and tear this ass out the frame, bend me over like this (illustrating by holding the bed rail with her hands together and leaning forward as if she would be touching her toes)." While spreading her legs, she peeps her head through, winks, and stands up finishing with, "But I don't think either of us can have what we'd like. It seems to me that your interview is over with officers." With a sly grin on her face, she ushered them out. "You can come back in the morning when she's rested if need be."

The officers came back a couple of days later following up because they had a few leads, but I was sedated. After they left the first interview, I was in so much pain the nurse gave me a sedative and morphine. I was in and out but constantly felt like shit.

I wake up in the same place I fell asleep. The damn hospital bed with a fucking catheter itching me like hell and an IV needle sticking me in my arm. The room is so quiet. It smells like a flower shop. A smell I love. It has pink walls with flowers around the top of the walls. And wow. No wonder it smells like a flower shop. I have a big bouquet of magnolias sitting on the end table, a dozen of white and pink roses on the vanity, and a bouquet of assorted flowers at the foot of my bed that need to be put in water. They're gorgeous. I pretend flowers don't matter on dates or throughout life period, but I secretly love them. I secretly from time to time buy red roses to bathe in. The smell puts me in a sensual mood and relaxed state of mind. See, I should have realized the date with John wouldn't end well because he didn't even bother to buy me flowers. I roll my eyes. John. The name is like a bad taste in my mouth. Like calf liver. Chalky. Bitter. Just utterly disgusting. I look over to my right and Janae is fast asleep in the chair. She's so beautiful. Her hair falls to her breasts in ringlets (it's her real hair too!) and her skin is a light chocolate brown. As uncomfortable as the chair looks, she's in a ball with one hand under her chin and the other between her legs sleeping like she hasn't a care in the world. I feel like I shouldn't wake her but my flowers really need water before they wither away. Who knows how long they have been sitting here.

"Nae Nae..." I say quietly, almost whispering. Nothing. She doesn't even move. That girl can sleep through a hurricane! I clear my throat. "Ahem! NAE NAE, wake up, love bug."

She jumps up. Startled at first, but then realizes it's me. "What? Are you okay? How you feeling? Do you need more pain meds? You hungry?" she says, agitated but full of concern. She looks like she hasn't slept in weeks. Poor thing has bags under her eyes and everything.

I inhale slowly. Lord knows I hadn't thought of either of those things. I just want to know when I can go home and have my flowers put in water. I now feel bad I've awakened her. So I figure I just slide my requests in. "You should go home and get some rest. I feel better. I love you. Oh, and uh, hey, before you leave, can you put my flowers in a vase with water?"

"You woke me up for that?! Bitch, you done lost it! I mean like really?! It's been a whole week and you wake up to tell me this shit? And Lord knows why Dev and some anonymous person keep bringing all these damn flowers like you dying or some shit! Smell like a damn funeral home in here! Flowers here, flowers over there, flowers at home, that's enough fucking flowers!" she says, showing how sleep-deprived she really is. I felt even worse now, knowing I had been the reason. But did she say Dev brought flowers? Wow! How sweet. I grin from ear to ear. Sweet ol Dev. But I wonder who the anonymous person is? Could it be John?

"A week?" I said, shocked, snapping back to reality realizing what she just said. I try to pretend I was unfazed knowing good and well the first thing now in my mind is school. What assignments have I missed? Will I be excused? Will they give me ample time to make up my work? What about tests? What am I going to do?

"Girl, yes, seven days. Your face and all the swelling is down and you're appearance is back to normal except for a couple bruises." I grab my face rubbing my cheeks. "You're okay, love. You're still as beautiful as ever." She smiles at me. "Thank God the swelling stopped." She smiles again. "You need to eat, though." She stands straightening her clothes as she's opening the door. "NURSE! She's woke. Can you send some food please?" I see a shadow through the blind-covered window nodding yes. "Thanks," says Janae as she closes the door. "I was wondering if you would wake up soon. I been giving you a bed bath twice a day, 'cause I don't trust them CNAs to do it right and been reading to you. But lawd, that chair was getting old!" she says, stretching her arms up high.

"You bathed me?" I asked.

"Well, yeah. Why? Didn't you need help dusting those cobwebs from down there?" she teased, pointing toward my private region.

OMG! That's embarrassing! "That's embarrassing!" I exclaimed.

"Girl," she said, waving her hands, "we got the same thing. You see one, you've seen 'em all! Shit, I was ready to slide on side of you in that bed. We small enough, it would've worked!" She said giggling, "But being it's been a whole week since I've had some, I decided not to. I'm too horny to have any skin-to-skin contact with anyone right now. Even if it's a girl! Then with all the spring cleaning, I had to do to get all the cobwebs out your who-ha—shit, it was just too much work! All I would've been able to do is turn over and go to sleep from exhaustion anyway!" We both laughed. She's a trip but she always has my back.

Chapter 3

Sigh. Home sweet home. On the drive back, Janae filled me in on what I missed the whole week I was in the hospital. Number 1, Janae went daily and picked up all my assignments for school. She also informed the dean about me being hospitalized, with doctor notes and excuses. She said the school was so concerned with my health, they wanted to allow me to be excused from all assignments and tests until further notice. Wow! Is all I could think. It was really amazing to know the teachers and the dean cared so much for me! Unfortunately, Janae said she told them she couldn't let them do that because they were already doing so much. DAMN JANAE! I was almost free!

Apparently "John" was ENGAGED to one of the girls that jumped me, and she was also the mother of his children. Shaking my head. There was nothing they could charge him for so he was free, but two of the three girls were arrested for assault and battery and attempted murder for having brass knuckles. They have since been released on bond. The other got off the hook because witnesses say she didn't touch me; she just recorded the incident on her phone. Which by the way is all over MySpace. I kind of knew he was too good to be true. I mean, he wasn't ALL that, but he had potential. Janae, on the other hand, found out who each girl was, where they lived and where they worked. The unbeweaveable one worked at a Starbucks on Canal St. where Janae sent her cousin Sean to flatten her tires, put sand in her tank, and write a little something on her car. Which was "Hope she was worth it, bitch!" and "This is just the beginning!" Each day consisted of some kind of disaster, which caused her to be in and out of the health clinic with a rash, four whole bean coffees thrown in her face, and fired by Thursday for filing a sexual harassment claim on her gay boss and pretending to know nothing about it. Haha. Sean is good! Poor thing. Didn't know what hit her. Her walls just came tumbling down overnight. She has no car, a rash she can't get rid of, and no job…

The girlfriend/baby mama/fiancé was found getting her hair done at Nappy Freedom Natural Hair Salon. She went in for a wash and flat iron but came out bald and had McDonald's arches for eyebrows. Thanks to Sean again! Haha. She left in an uproar of course but ended up having to take a cab because her car wouldn't start. It was probably sand in her tank as well. I'm not sure. The taxi driver didn't speak English, or so he said, ended up dropping her off in seventh ward, which should've been St. Benard. (No one wants to get dropped off anywhere near the seventh ward in New Orleans. It's a sub-district of the mid-city district area of New Orleans. Its overall crime rate is 110 percent higher than the national average). Meanwhile, CPS was at her house picking up her three-month-old son, and one-year-old son, which she had left home alone with her ten-year-old daughter and sister, who had been lured around the block by one of Seans boys with the promise of a shopping spree. Supposedly the baby mom is still trying to get a ride home and her kids are in foster care.

We arrive home, and as we walk in the door, I say, "Janae, I think I will go take a hot bath…" I hear a loud gasp as I turn down the hall walking to my room.

"JAZMYNN, oh my God, I'm so glad you're okay! I've been missing you around here." I hear a voice that's oh so familiar. It was Devon. Devon Edward motherfucking Thomas. The finest thing you'll ever see. Arms stretched wide, awaiting a hug. He was a dear friend to me and Janae. When we go out, he's like our bodyguard. He won't let a guy get next to us unless we say otherwise. Janae says we make a cute couple, but I don't think he likes me like that. He is sexy for a Caucasian guy. That curly black hair with them green eyes—OMG! He's tanned year round, and boy, do I love this time of the year because he's usually shirtless showing his well-chiseled abs. God, he's yummy!

"Hey, hunk," I say as I close into his embrace. He smells of Kenneth Cole Black a personal favorite of mine. His hugs always make me feel so secure and safe.

"How are you feeling?" he asks. I can hear the concern in his voice. It's not like when a person asks that question because something happened and they're supposed to. It was sincere and genuine. "A whole lot better. I think I will feel even better after I submerge my ass in water and take a hot bath."

"Already ready for you" he whispers in my ear before gently letting me go.

"Already ready?!" I exclaimed.

"Yeah, Nae Nae called and said you were coming home so I took the liberty of running your bath."

"Well, that was really sweet and thoughtful, thanks, Devon. I will be out in a few y'all." I say heading toward the bathroom.

As I walk into the bathroom, I'm taken by surprise. The lights are off but the glow of candles fills the bathroom. There are candles up the steps of the garden tub and all around it. The smell of jasmine fills the air. A smell I also love. The tub is filled to the brim with bubbles as the sound of Luther Vandross plays on the radio. My God, Dev is so thoughtful. There's a wine bucket with a bottle of what looks like white Zinfandel and two glasses beside it. Two glasses? Does he think I'm an alcoholic?! Smiling, I undress and enter the tub. The water is perfect. There's a knock at the door. Ensuring my body is covered with bubbles, I say, "Come in," expecting Janae.

Devon enters. I blush. "You did all this for me?" I ask quietly.

"Anything for you. I feel so bad I couldn't protect you when that shit happened to you. I visited you the first few days, but I couldn't take seeing you hurt like that anymore. Especially knowing I wasn't there to protect you." Is that a tear in his eye? I know not! He looks away. "It's fine, Dev. I'm okay now." Looking back at me, "Would you like me to wash your back?" He said flirtatiously.

"Um…only if you pour me a glass of wine first and massage my feet and…" Before I could finish.

"Done." He smiles as he rolls up his pants leg. I blush again. Does this dude know what he does to me? I doubt it. I sit up as he climbs in behind me covering my breasts with my washcloth. He gets in and he grabs my shoulders and gently leads me back between his knees. He leans over to grab the bottle of wine and I flinch. He begins pouring us each a glass. Hell, I thought he was about to grab my breasts! He hands me my glass, toasts his to mine, saying, "Welcome back home!" and then takes a sip. He then grabs my bottle of jasmine soap, squeezes a boatload into his hands, and starts massaging my neck and shoulders. I hope he knows he's buying another bottle. That shit ain't cheap. It's meant to be used in moderation! I moan. It feels so good. Okay, never mind about buying another bottle. This shit worth it! R Kelly is playing on the radio "I don't see nothing wrong, with a little bump and grind…" He massages to the beat and I'm getting heated. His hands feel so good! I want them all over me. My breasts began to throb wanting to be massaged too. By his mouth! Oh, them lips. I lick my lips. He digs deeper into my shoulders. Taking every ache, worry, and thought away. This is so relaxing… After what felt like a min (but was actually about forty minutes), he taps me. "Take your bath you're turning into a prune. I will massage your feet when you get out."

And just like that, he was done. I sigh sleepily. "Okay." He gently pushes me up and gets out. Dries his feet and leaves. I feel like a boiled spaghetti noodle. Relaxed and limp. I finish up, wrap myself in my towel, and exit to my bedroom. He's there waiting with lotion in hand. "Lay down." I do as I'm told and lie down on my stomach. He walks to the head of the bed, leans down, and kisses my forehead. "Relax" he whispers. He goes back to the foot of the bed and sits then began to lotion my feet, on up to my calves, under the towel to my thighs. Feels like heaven. But for some strange reason, I'm exhausted. I can barely keep my eyes open. I began to doze off into a relaxing state of mind until I'm sound asleep.

I wake to the smell of fried chicken. A personal favorite. I yawn and stretch as I roll out of bed. I'm still in my towel from my bath!

Awe shit. I slept through my massage. Whelp guess that means Imma have to request another. The full body this time! I throw on under clothes and a blue-jean romper and walk into the living room. The TV is blasting that new video "Sweet Love" by Chris Brown, and Nae Nae is dancing by the stove. She looks up with her gorgeous smile. "Hey, sleepyhead, you hungry?"

"Lawd, yes. I could eat a leg or two." I giggle. "Where's Dev?" As I look around. "On a date. Said he will be back if she got hoe tendencies." She laughed. "Dat boy a trip," she says while shaking her head.

What the hell? "A date?! With who?" I say, instantly jealous. "Oh, jus' some uppity bitch from uptown. It ain't gone last, just like all the rest of them. You do know he's jus' waitin for you to come to your senses, huh?" She winks, and I quickly turn defensive, "Uh, no. I am so not his type."

Although deep inside I'm wishing it's true. "Girl, stop playing. You know damn well that boy in love with you! He only goes on the dates to piss you off! And besides, he ain't never ran my bath water or massaged my feet till I fell asleep. Hmm. Sounds like love right thur. I heard them slow jams playing in the bathroom too…" She brings the food she's prepared to the table for us to eat. Fried chicken with garlic potatoes. Corn on the cob, garlic bread, and steamed broccoli. Yummy! I begin licking my lips. If I didn't know how much my bestie loved me, I do now!

Chapter 4

It has been a few weeks since my hospital visit. It's the day of graduation, and my birthday is tomorrow. I'm so excited. I will finally have my PhD in counseling. As I lay my leopard-print spaghetti-strap, knee-length dress on the bed, I can't help but wonder what Dev has been up to. We hadn't talked in a few days. He didn't come back after his date on Tuesday, so I guess unfortunately it went well. I take a deep breath while walking to my full-body-length mirror. My body and hair is still wet from my shower. I grab my towel and dry my body off, and then began to apply my skin so soft body oil, still watching myself in the mirror.

I would say I'm what a lot of men would want. Sort of the model body type. I'm five-foot-three, I weigh about 130 pounds with perky 34-C cupped breasts. My stomach is flat and although you can't sit a drink on my ass, it still sticks out. My hair is naturally straight and hangs tickling my nipples as I move. I look at the time. It's 3:15 p.m. I don't have to be at the school for graduation until 5:45 p.m. Sighing, I was staring at myself in the mirror, when I hear a knock at the door. *Knock, knock.* Before I can answer I hear one more knock on the door then Dev waltz in. He throws me on the bed and runs his hands up and down my body, rubbing the excess oil in. What the hell? I'm speechless and can't say a word. The door! I say to myself. Is it locked?! I quickly get up and run to my door and double-check the lock to ensure I have no intruders. If we are about to do this, I'm ready. Really ready! He grabs me once again and throws me to the bed this time saying, "Stay!" I close my eyes and he begins to tongue my left nipple in a circular motion. Slowly at first squeezing the nipple here and there with his lips until I feel a tingle. I'm beginning to feel a strange sensation that I've never felt before. It's amazing! My body screams for more. Before I know it he's already entered my lady garden with his finger. The way I'm feeling has me high on ecstasy. He pushes in and out slowly while moving down and tickling my leaves, making me want to let go, but not yet. What is he doing? I've never seen a scene like this on any of the porn I've watched! He tugs at my right breast, not wanting it to get jealous of the left.

"OH, Devon." He's so fine. So muscular. "You don't know how long I've been wanting this. Not to mention wanting this with YOU! Get on top of me!" I scream. "Make love to me. Give me your pleasure rod."

He does. He starts off slow, sliding his pole from one inner wall to the next. He then starts moving his pleasure rod a little faster in and out. That's right, Dev. Right there. Tug at one breast while kissing on the other! I yell. Faster and deeper he goes with that big pole. In and out. In and out. "Oh, Devon, I love you!" I'm about to release every ounce of juice my body has all over his big pole.

"I love you too, baby," he whispers. And we begin to release. Together. In a fury of clouds. I'm loud, I know I am, but I don't give a fuck. This shit here is the shit! The convulsions. The way our bodies vibrate together. Ecstacy! The sticky sweet smell of sex. I fucking love it. It doesn't even bother me it lasted like two seconds. It's really hard to move. I don't want this moment or feeling to end! He eventually rolls over and lets out a sigh. I hope he liked it. I sure did. I lay motionless with my eyes closed for a good five minutes with a big smile on my face. I'm weak and can't move, but a good weak. I'm in a feeling of sweet bliss…

I wake up stretching, never realizing I fell asleep. I feel so relaxed. "What's that noise?" I ask Dev. Reaching over to tap his arm. "Dev?" I tap nothing but a pillow. I open my eyes and look toward my left in the area I hear the noise and find it. My vibrator under my dry towel. The hell is this doing here? I wonder. I lay back and close my eyes again. That was the most amazing feeling ever! I click off the vibrator and reopen my eyes. I look toward the right side of the bed Dev was in, and he's gone. Maybe he went to the restroom to shower? I get up, wrap my towel around me, and head to the bathroom. Nothing. "Well, maybe he showered and went to his room?" I wonder aloud. I went down the hall through the kitchen and knock on Dev's door. No answer. Wow! Did he just skip out on me? Was I that bad? I scratch my head as I turn to head back toward my room. I notice the front door is locked. Dev never locks the door. That is something me and Janae continuously fuss at him about because he says he always forget, and we always tell him one day he's going to forget and someone will be in here waiting on one of us to rob us when we get home! This is crazy, but I guess I will have to figure it out later because it's time to dress and get ready for my graduation.

I head back to the bathroom to quickly shower again. As I look at myself in my full-length mirror, I notice my bed is in the same condition it was when I first showered beside the few wrinkles on the left side of the bed I woke up on. I'm really beginning to think Dev's not here and I don't think he ever was…

The day I've been waiting for since I began college. Graduation. I'm sitting waiting to get my name called to go get my diploma and, of course, see my two favorite people. Nae Nae and Dev. Behind them, I see a guy who looks familiar but can't really place him. Nae Nae and Dev are smiling and waving away. I've made them proud, and I love it. It's something I aim for every day in life being my mom never really cared. I look at Dev. I decide I have to tell Devon about how I feel before it's too late. I can only hope he will feel the same way. But then again if he does, why hasn't he made the first move? I frown at the thought of rejection. I will probably cry my eyes out. And for what? Something that never was? "JAZMYNN OLIVIA BARKLEY!" I hear over the loudspeaker. I gracefully walk and receive my diploma holding tears from the fear of rejection shaking each professor hand mouthing "thank you" to each. They probably think I'm emotional because of how big this day is, but they are completely wrong. I hear clapping and whistling and of course Nae Nae over everything "THAT'S MY BEST FREIND YALL!" I giggle as I return to my seat. She is my biggest supporter!

Nae Nae takes a million pictures of me before she allows me to take off my graduation gown. I don't mind it at all. I love the camera. I just hate that damn gown. It does nothing for my figure. Just looks like some long ass robe I'm wearing singing in the choir at church.

Nae Nae said, "Well, ma'am, what do you want to do tonight?" As I'm finally taking off that stupid oversized church girl gown.

"I don't care, really. What do y'all feel like doing?" Devon grabs me from behind picking me up. "Put me down, dammit! This dress is already short as hell!" I said sternly trying to let him know I was joking. After swinging me around, he finally does. Grinning his dazzling smile from ear to ear, while I'm pulling my dress back down to a decent level.

"Shut yo ass up, you know you like it," Nae Nae says while rolling her eyes.

"Congrats! You did it!" Dev said, overly excitedly. Rubbing his hands together, "What are we doing tonight?"

We?! What? Dev, just do me! Thumps my vagina. Quit playing games, bruh! I'm looking at him with a fuck-me face and need to recuperate quickly. Say something, say something! "Let's go to Vegas!" I say, not really knowing where it came from. I mean, I told myself to say something, but Vegas?

"VEGAS?!" They both say in unison in disbelief.

"Yes, Vegas," I say more confidently this time. I decided that would be the best place to tell Dev how I feel about him… I have to say something. I need closure or confirmation!

Chapter 5

We arrive in Vegas in three hours and twenty minutes after finally finishing packing for a week. Truthfully, Janae and I have so much luggage you would've thought we were moving. That's what women do though, right? El Cortez (our hotel) was nice. Especially for the fact we went for the cheapest possible being we knew we would never stay in the room. Man, to say we had the cabana junior suite, it was still awesome! More than awesome. Me and Nae Nae have our own rooms with adjoining doors to one of the bathrooms and Dev is on one of the couches. Chuckling to myself, or maybe with me. Maybe. The thought came back to mind my true reason for coming here and what I day-dreamed before graduation. I can't fucking believe I feel so deeply about him and he doesn't even know. My birthday is at midnight. Did I want the rejection just yet?! Nah. Probably not... Nah, I don't think so.

We unpacked excitedly. This will be the trip of our lives!

Dev said, "Soooo, what's on the agenda, Jazmynn?" smacking on some grapes he brought from our house.

I replied, "Well, I'm not quite sure yet... See I didn't quite think this all through, and..."

Nae Nae said, "Bitch, jus' tell him!" I jump. Felt like ten feet high. I'm scared out my wits. Wide eyes and all! How did she know what we were coming for?! Before I could open my mouth she says "We celebrating! Shit, we gone party till the lights go out! Then come on again. Then go back out. We gonna jus' keep going till we pass out and don't know where the fuck we are! Baaaaaahahahaha." She walks to the kitchen laughing hysterically.

PHEW! I thought she knew! Good grief! Bullet dodged! Shit, I need to turn the AC up in here. I broke out in a sweat real quick. Whoo Saaa…

Nae Nae said, "Shit, we partying til the sunrise, and popping bottles till we too drunk to open them! Bitch, I hope you didn't think I forgot?!"

"Forgot? Forgot what?" acting innocent. I know she hasn't forgotten about my birthday. Hell, she reminds me of my birthday. But I'm so worried she's about to spill the beans and embarrass me.

Throwing her hands up, "Nah, she tryna play coy and shit"—shaking her head—"your birthday, hoe!"

Phew! "Nae Nae, why you gotta be so vulgar? You ain't gotta call me all them bitches and shit. What if I constantly called you a bitch?"

"Muafucka, I wouldn't give a damn! Long as you put 'BAD' in front of it!" Snapping her fingers in the air. "What's got yo panties in a wad?!" Putting my head down looking at my hands. "Nothing. I'm jus' saying, though you be trippi…"

"All right, all right, y'all calm y'all asses down. Let's not have any 'bitchfits'"—doing the quotations with his fingers. "Let's go have some fun and TURN UP! It's time to celebrate a graduate and another year of life!" We all burst into laughter. I know Nae Nae has my back through whatever, but her name calling pisses me off. We are going to have to talk about it soon before I blow up. She needs to respect me more.

As Nae Nae and I are dressing in the master bathroom (being that women need more space of course), Dev gets dressed in the other. I wish I was a fly on the wall. I'm not quite sure how well they can see, but hopefully, if I was that fly, I could see every angle and even get a taste! Nae Nae is almost done putting on her face while I'm just sitting staring at my reflection in the mirror. I was never one to wear makeup. I feel like I have that natural beauty that doesn't need it. I say that, but honestly, don't know the correct way to apply everything. I put a little lipstick, eyeliner, and mascara and go.

Then I hear a knock at the door.

"Please tell me none of y'all idiots ordered room service!?" Rolling my eyes. Getting ready to walk toward the door.

Nae Nae said, "What the fuck?! Why not?" As I frown with disapproval, she says "nah girl not me" still playing with her lashes.

"It's for me!" Dev yells. "I got it." Now I'm furious. Best believe he's paying for that shit! I ain't playing… Then I hear a female's voice… 'Ugh! It took FOREVER to load the plane! I didn't think I would make it!' She sounds like she is doing her best at an English accent, but you can still hear the African American in her."

"Oh, it's okay, Makailah, come in and make yourself comfortable my friends are still getting ready. You know how you women can be." He laughs, calling himself making a joke. Hardy Har! Nosy me walks out of the room to see a bitch you can tell thought she was all that and a bag of chips. She looks familiar, like I may have seen her before but, then again, I don't know the hoe. She was wearing some blue skinny jeans with a silver metallic spaghetti strapped shirt and pink heels. Somebody should've given her the memo that if you got thick thighs, a belly and your belly sticks out further than your booty do, wear looser clothing. Looking worse than sponge bob! Like someone vomited Pepto Bismol on her feet. Girl, get the fuck out of here! Grant it, I have nothing against plus-sized or thick women. I just feel the ones that try to dress like they're a size 2 and they forget the "0" should be arrested by the fashion police for attempting to wear rubber bands in public. I look over to Dev and he's smiling harder than a punk with a bag full of dicks he got in his stocking for Christmas! What in THE fuck?! Who the fuck is this bitch?!

"Jazzy, this is Makailah." He reaches out his hands as if he's auctioning off a car on *The Price Is Right*. I am now livid. Is he trying to ruin my night? My birthday? Which is it? By now I can probably spit fire. Is he calling himself mocking me? This is some bullshit! Didn't this afternoon mean shit to you? Wait, that wasn't real… But shit, it felt so real. Damn bastard! "You know fucking well I don't like being called that. And who the fuck IS she? Better yet, what in the fuck is she doing here?"

Makailah looks like she already knows shit is about to get real. Her jaw dropped and eyes are wide. She better not say shit to me.

The more I stare at her the more familiar she is to me. "I'm sorry, I can go…" she says as she starts to grab her clutch off of the couch. This hoe in here seriously getting comfortable and shit. For the life of me, I can't get out of my head why she looks so damned familiar.

"Please do!" Motioning my hand toward the door.

"JAZMYNN!" Devon says with the most puzzled face I've ever seen.

"Motherfucker, don't JAZMYNN me! Who the fuck is this?!" He answers with his arms outstretched, the dumbest explanation in life. "A friend of mine. We went on a couple dates. I didn't think you would mind, or more less give a fuck! Because we are only friends." His face is now furious. I couldn't tell if it was my reaction or the situation or what. He starts pacing the floor. I can't take looking at him anymore. The longer I stand here, the more I want to burst into tears. "It sure the hell would've been good having a heads up, FRIEND!" I stormed away hearing an argument break out between the two.

Makailah asked, "What the hell is going on, Devon?"

Dev answered, "Man nothing, she's fucking tripping."

Makailah said, "Clearly, something is! If I were a stranger I would think you guys were in a relationship! Like, damn, dude! She's pissed the fuck off because I'm here like ya'll fucking or something! Homegirl looks a little familiar too!"

Dev, silencing her, said, "Nah, it nothing like that. I think she jus' got so much on her plate she's aggravated. Lemme go talk to her real quick, I'll be right back. I really apologize for her actions."

I try to squeeze back into the bathroom, but Nae Nae closes the door. "Nae Nae, don't do this to me! Please!" I whisper. And there he is… Even more handsome mad. It would be so awesome to have makeup sex right now. That is if we were together. Which we aren't. So that can't happen. Or can it? Snap back, Jazmynn! "Girl, answer me! Imma need you to please, please explain what all that bullshit was for!"

"Bullshit?!" I ask, clueless. Don't look him in the eye. Don't do it! "Girl, your birthday is in a few hours, and I ain't tryna mess it up." He turns around, putting his hands on his hips. "But…" He turns back to me. He walks close. Too close for comfort. He grabs my chin and points my face to his, and makes me look into those gorgeous green eyes. "You got some explaining to do."

And that's it! It's all I can take! I tiptoe, inch in, and kiss him. My tongue against his. Going back and forth. He tastes of spearmint. He pushes me away and stares at me, questioning, "What the hell is going on?" My eyes tear up, and as soon as I went to walk away, he grabs me around my waist and pulls me close and this time he initiates the tongue war. Ugh! There goes my flowers ruffling up in my lady garden again! I wrap my arms around his waist. He takes a handful of my ass. Spreading my cheeks a little. Never had that done before, but I like it. I pull my arms up and wrap my arms around his neck. He stops the passionate kiss. Again, but only for a split second. While looking into my eyes, he then grabs the back of my neck with his other hand and gives me something deeper. Something I've never felt before. LOVE. He's kissing me so hard and passionately that I need a breath, but it isn't worth missing another second of this!

GASP! We jump. Both in a daze. I'm hating our moment has stopped, but, shit. It's Janae.

Janae said, "Well, I be damned. 'Bout time! We still going out tonight though huh? I don't mind being a third wheel. Y'all jus' save the tonguing down and lovemaking part till we get back to the room. Or y'all wanna go ahead and get that part out the way now? It's still early. Dev prob' ain' nothing but a minute man anyway…"

"SHHH!" we say in unison. I honestly don't know why I did it because I already know that means talk louder to Janae. "Don't shush me! What YALL doin?!" Really loud. Like, she should be a human loudspeaker loud.

I turn and run to the bathroom in tears of embarrassment. What the hell was I thinking! He has a date in the living room! I really don't give a fuck about her, but I know it's wrong and I wouldn't want it done to me. I can hear Dev say out to me, "Jazmynn, wait! JAZMYNN!" But I've already fled the scene. All I can think is what the hell have I done? Tonight was not supposed to be the night to let him know how I feel. At least not yet! I needed a few drinks to down first or something! Now I've done this, and will have explaining to do in a few.

Janae said, "Ooooooo! Don't you have some business to tend to?" She points behind him. Stunned, Makailah is standing in the doorway face red with furry and arms crossed. She must have seen the whole thing too. "Really, Devon? I thought y'all were just friends? I can't believe I brought my dumbass all the way over here thinking you liked me and this was a chance to get to know each other better! I could've kept the money I paid my babysitter and for this damn flight!" As she's grabbing her bags, she's placed by one of the sofas (this bitch just knew she was going to stay and party with us) he runs to her apologetically. "Makailah, I'm so sorry. You have to believe me. There's nothing going on between us. I don't know what the hell just happened. We are just friends."

Makailah said, "No, Devon. There was more there. I saw it for myself. That was fucked up. Ugh! I can't stand men, and I definitely need to move! It's always the same shit with the basic bitches! Just so you know, I liked your brother. He said he wasn't interested and referred me to you because of your sex appeal. You got sex appeal all right. Imma cuss his ass out soon as I see him!" Then she storms out leaving Devon running his hand through his hair.

Janae popping her gum says, "Bye, bitch! Bye!" smiling from eye to ear. "So what now? What you gonna do? You got a brother? Since when? He looks like you, or you the cute one? Is he single? We can double date! You know what? Don't worry about it right now. Point is, you're in love with JAZMYNN and you know it. Why you brought that bitch here knowing that would upset JAZMYNN? Then have the audacity to kiss her? What the fuck are you thinking about? Answer me, Dev!" she yells.

"I can't deal with this right now, Nae Nae. I don't have no brother, he's dead. Man, fuck this shit. I'm out. Imma catch up with y'all later," grabbing his blazer off the chair by the door he walks out. Janae ran to the door and yelled out, "And where the hell exactly you planning on going in sin city without us? I know damn well you ain't 'bout to run after that bitch…with her raggedy ass weave!"

"Janae Christian, I jus' need some fresh air to clear my head. My head all fucked up right now! I really don't feel like this bullshit! Not now!" he said as he walked down the hotel hallway. Nae Nae knows when Dev says her first name, he's upset so she decides to let it go for time being. "Well, all right hit us up. Be careful, and don't take too long. We 'bout ready to go, I think." He chucked up the peace sign and rounded the corner completely out of sight.

I'm staring at myself in the mirror. Eyes red and swollen. My lips flush red. From that kiss I guess. That kiss. Mmm…it was even better than I could ever imagine! But I'm so confused! He kissed me back! He could've pushed me away! Well, he kind of did, but then he gave me more than I gave him! So then why would he invite some chick over and then kiss me like that? He wanted me. I know he did. He had too. I could feel his pleasure rod harden between us. I wanted him. All of him. He wanted me just as bad as I wanted him. His body said so. The door cracks open. "Can I come in?" asks Janae.

"Yeah," I say as I sigh.

"What the hell was that?"

"Man, I don't even know." I chuckle. It was it! It was real! It was, unanswered…I decide to change out of what I was wearing and wear something else. Something a little more comfortable.

As I'm moving around the room, pairing an outfit together, Janae asks, "Well are you okay?" She's always concerned about my well-being. She's so strong. It's like nothing ever happens to her. I admire her strength and hope to someday be as strong as she is. I dry my eyes with the back of my hand, "I will be. Y'all ready?" I attempt to gain the strength Janae always show.

"Well, Dev left to clear his head he said. And he said he will hit us up later." She sounded like she really didn't believe a word that came out of her own mouth, but was trying to convince me. She's pissed too. I frown, wondering if the chick is with him or if he ran after her. Breathing deeply "Okay, well let's go party! I wanna get fucked up." Better yet I need to get fucked up!

Chapter 6

There are so many people out here, it is ridiculous! We were going from casino to casino when we finally roll up on Dev at the Palazzo. He was sitting at a craps tables with a shit load of chips. He looked like he was in deep thought. God, he's handsome. He had on a black polo shirt I liked with light-colored, stone-washed jeans and some black polo shoes. His hair curly as always; he's clean shaven and is wearing that beautiful smile. There was a gorgeous woman standing next to him playing as well. She kept flipping her hair and nudging him trying to keep his attention, but he seemed completely uninterested especially soon as he saw me. A guy with long straight hair and a weird-looking beard walks away from the table behind Dev as we were walking up. He gives me a little half smile. His eyes look familiar. I wanted to ask him if he liked what he saw, but that would've sounded a little conceited. I voted against it. Dev smiled as we approached him approvingly. Nae Nae was dressed in a full-body shorts bodysuit with tie-up heels. I, on the other hand, thought I would go for a more relaxed look with distressed jeans that fit just right, a red-lace half-shirt top that showed my belly and a lot of cleavage, and some red bottom heels. I had decided to change out of the dress I had on last minute because I thought if Dev didn't really want me, he would at least be able to see what he's missing!

"Hey, beautiful ladies." He stands and kisses Nae Nae's hand and reaches for mine, but I turn away looking across the casino, folding my arms as if I never saw his gesture. He grabs me around the waist anyway and whispers in my ear, "We need to talk. But tonight is about you. It's your birthday. If you don't want me here I can leave." Turning me around gently while looking at me from head to toe. He bites his bottom lip, making me bite mine. He is so delicious!

"No, stay," I say with a half-smile.

"You sure?" he asks, grinning, showing his sparkling white teeth. "Yes, I'm sure."

He turns around to Nae Nae. "Let's get this party started! As you can tell ladies"—reaching over, grabbing his chips and putting them in a complimentary bag—"I had a good bit of luck. EVERYTHING is on me tonight." Shaking his bag, making the chips jingle, he turns back to me. "So first things first birthday girl. Let's go eat!" He puts his left arm around Nae Nae's shoulder and the right around mine. Kisses me sweetly on the temple and gives me a wink. That makes me blush and melt every time.

We ate our bellies full of fried shrimp, chicken strips, and the night really began. We bounced from casino to casino, drinking shot after shot. We would put a dollar or two in machines we felt and move around to other ones. Here and there we would hit a jackpot, cash out, and try the same machine again. If we had no luck, we took a shot. If we had luck we took a shot. Later, we decided we were tired of the casinos and decided to stop to a few nightclubs. At 3:00 a.m. I finally suggested we go back to the room. It was my birthday day. It should be a national holiday, but I'm working on that. I took some Dramamine and Aleve to avoid waking up with a headache or a hangover. I definitely didn't want to sleep all day and be sick on my day. I called it a night. Dev and Nae Nae played the radio and danced around like crazy. Two drunks I chuckle. I'm worried about being able to celebrate my birthday later, and I just may be celebrating by myself, because they will be the ones hungover. I love them two till the death of me though…

"Rise and shine, birthday girl!" Dev says quietly while holding a tray of assorted fruits, bagels, and cream cheese.

"It's time to get up." He winks. Dude, can you at least let me get myself together before you just barge in talking about rise and shine? I haven't even brushed my teeth yet, and Lord knows what I look like right about now! I yawn and stretch causing the covers to fall below my breasts. He blushes as he sits the tray down, never taking his eyes off me. I look down, forgetting I'm only in my bra and panties and hurry to pull the covers back up. "Take a picture, it'll last longer!" I snort while grabbing a strawberry.

He sits on the edge of the bed, snickering, "I already have!" I laugh, too, because I really don't mind him looking. Poor thing isn't the best of flirters though.

Dev said, "I watched you sleep for a few minutes. You're so beautiful when you sleep. I know that's kind of awkward…but I couldn't resist. You do the cutest things when you sleep. You smile, giggle, your eyes roll back from time to time, but you know…" cutting his sentence off. "Hey, can we talk?"

And here it goes… The moment I've been waiting for and dreading at the same time. Does he want to talk about last night? Of course, he does! Oh, good grief! He watched me sleep? Why?! I can't. I just can't! How do I start?

"Jazmynn, are you okay?!" I shake back to reality out of my thoughts.

Nodding meekly, "Yes, yes I'm fine."

He looks unsure if he's ready to talk himself. "So… Can we talk?"

Pretending I'm lost about the situation, "About what?" I say, avoiding his glorious green eyes grabbing another strawberry. He begins looking a little annoyed, "Don't play coy now, we need to hurry and have this conversation so we can all get ready to start our wonderful day. But what was up with you last night? You pretend to have no interest in Devon, and next thing I know you're tonguing him down! I don't understand! What was up with that? And I know today's your birthday, and I don't want to ruin your day…" We hear someone walking outside the door. Holding a finger in the air, like he has just thought of a bright idea. "You know what?"—he claps his hands together—"never mind, we can talk about it later…" He heads toward the bathroom which has an adjuring door to Janae's room…

I stand to my feet, wrapping my body with the sheets. Careful not to show too much skin and my emotions at the same time. I'm unsure what to say! I don't even know how to say it! How do you tell the person you're in love with you are madly in love, without knowing if you will be rejected or not? But that kiss… It was so intimate. I saw sparks! I felt my body tremble. I fell lost in his kiss. I felt loved…

There's a knock at my door. I answer, "Come in!" He's back. Guess he changed his mind and wants to talk now. He sighs a deep breath. Mumbles "Good morning," and says, "We need to talk about last night, I'm so hungover, but we need to do this right now."

"You want to talk now?" I ask.

"Yes," he answers. "What was up with you last night? What does this mean?" He starts running his hand through his hair and pacing the floor. "I'm at a loss for words. I don't know what to think or how to feel!" He stops at the doorway and says, "Well are you going to answer me? I feel I do deserve an answer, Jazmynn."

I turn and face him. He seems to get more and more beautiful every day. Okay. Deep breath. Here it goes… "I don't know, Dev. I love you…I mean I like you…I mean like… Yesterday before graduation was amazing!" Oh, God! I shouldn't have said that! I must sound ridiculous.

He begins smiling from ear to ear. Love? That's a strong word. A word most guys run from because of the fear of commitment. Completely different in this case. He looked happy, confused, and angry at the same time. I tried to keep the river from flowing from my eyes, but the dam is breaking. "I understand I may not be your type and I apologize for messing up whatever you had with what's her name. I don't know what came over me. I just, I… Jesus Christ! Will you say something?!" The tears are trickling down my face in a steady stream now. The day of rejection is here! It's confirmed. How could I have been so stupid? Why for any moment would I think he would want me? What do I have to offer him? All those pretty girls he dates. I can't compete! I'm a virgin for God sakes! I don't even have any sexual experience. Well, not anymore, but I…I don't know how…I just… Ugh! How does a person fall in love with another person who…

"Jazmynn, calm down…" he says as he walks over to me. I'm sobbing uncontrollably now. As I look up at his gorgeous face, I notice his eyes were a little watery too. "Girl, I've loved you since the first time I laid eyes on you in the mall." Wrapping me up in his arms.

"I thought YOU had no interest in me! I wasn't sure how to approach you with my feelings being that you always kindly pushed me aside and seemed uninterested. I really thought you were too good for me. How can I cop such an intelligent, beautiful, sophisticated woman like you? Girl, this is music to my ears! This is the best day of my life! The feelings are beyond mutual. So if you would..." As he loosens his grasp and takes a step back. "Will you date me?" he whispers while reaching for my left hand. With that sexy half smile and those green eyes to die for. I stifle a giggle through the tears. I realize he's kind of corny too. I pick up my right hand and reach for his.

"Definitely!"

He comes in and embraces me with his strong arms. Now standing face-to-face, my eyes to his nose. He gently reaches down and lifts my chin. I can barely breathe. The things I'm feeling in my stomach right now! My heart's in my throat. He leans in and presses his lips to mine. His lips taste of sweet strawberries and I feel my body melt away. He kisses well. (Not that I've kissed many frogs in my day.) I chuckle. He stops. Looking me in the eyes as though he sees through my entire soul. "Was that weak? Or am I that bad?" he asks. "Umm...kinda weak," I say playfully.

He then grabs my face with both hands. "Oh, I can do better!" And begins kissing me so deeply, so intimately, so...

"Oh, ah...ah!" says a voice that's oh so familiar. "Y'all not doing this shit again, huh? Man, look, why don't y'all just start dating already? Ya'll both in love with each other and Y'all know it. Aye! BIRTHDAY SEX, BIRTHDAY SEX..." She starts singing and dancing around the room.

We let go of each other and turn to look at her. She's winding her ass in a circle snapping her fingers while grinning from ear to ear. We all burst into laughter. She's a character!

Chapter 7

As I look at myself in the mirror, I come to the realization I just might be pretty. I mean my self-confidence is pretty high, but after a few failed dates, I was beginning to wonder if I was loveable. And it dawned on me, am I relationship material? Then I came out with the truth to Dev how I felt about him. I just might be all that and more! I mean, someone actually wants and loves me! I recently bought some makeup to wear for my graduation ceremony. Which I ended up not wearing for lack of knowledge on how to apply it. Well, there will be no need for it now! I have a man! I chuckle to myself. It's still unbelievable. The man I dreamed of. The man I wished for. My everything! I'm in a total bliss. Besides all that, I can't quit thinking about the fact he will eventually be fucking my brains out on the regular. I'm so ready. Like ready, ready.

I finish flat ironing my hair with my wonderful Sedu Ionic Ceramic Tourmaline Straightener, add a little Bobbie Brown Fire lip gloss, and stand and look at my reflection. That iridescent pink gloss on my lips makes me look like a lip model in Vogue. My cute little pink-and-white spaghetti-strapped floral print sundress fits me so well. It hugs my breasts and puts them on a wonderful display, while the bottom of the dress flares a little, giving more oomph to my ass. I twirl a little in the mirror admiring what God has given me, then I grab my shades while slipping on some flip-flops, grab my two-piece swimsuit, bag, and sunscreen as I head to the door.

Nae Nae is applying her face as always. I say applying her face because she uses some shit I thought was used for paint. The fuck is primer? "You ready?" I ask. She's soooooo pretty and doesn't even need makeup, but I have to say that her makeup is always so perfect. She has a real talent for it. The things she does to make her eyes pop! It's so sad she doesn't realize how much money she's wasting, though. I think she pays for the name of the cosmetics because the products don't look any different than the ones at the dollar stores. "Yes, indeed, love!" She smiles. Her teeth are perfect. I've only known her about five years now, but I always wondered if she ever had braces before we met.

"So where's Dev?" I ask. Where my man at? With his fine self. I wore one of my best perfumes just for him. Burberry Weekend. I smile inwardly. I know from experience guy's love that fragrance. Although it hasn't landed me a husband just yet, I know inwardly one day it will!

"He's gonna meet us at the pool later." She stands as she lines her under eye liner up with her finger in the mirror. "He said he had something to do real quick. I don't know what the fuck he got to do out here, 'cause he doesn't know any fucking body out here. At least that we know of." She says to me looking out of the corner of her eye. "So what's up with y'all? You finally tell him how you in love with him and how badly you want to screw his brains out? How you masturbate thinking of him and how you really want the d?" She says with a huge smirk on her face. I swear I don't know why the fuck I tell her everything. I need to start keeping personal shit personal. "Come on, spill the beans. I know it's not a coincidence Y'all getting caught kissing two times in a row. I ain't no fool."

I giggle like a little school girl. She is a character! I guess that's why we're friends and have maintained such a strong relationship. Honesty is the key. "I guess we're dating…" I said, shrugging my shoulders and turning away acting as though its nothing, knowing I don't know how to contain my relief and happiness. Nae Nae looks at me with her big brown eyes serious as a heart attack, "If he hurts you, I will kill him! We cool, but we ain't that cool. You come first. Nobody else will hurt you. I promise you that!" Stretching open her arms while walking over to me. "He's my boy, but you are my sister," she says with a serious face that kind of scared me. "Bring it in, bestie, better yet sister, 'cause we waaaaay more than just friends!" We embrace in a twenty-second hug. She loves me and only wants the best, but she's almost like an overprotective boyfriend sometimes. I know one thing; she ain't letting shit happen to me unless I want it to if she can help it. Maybe that's why my love for her is so strong and vice versa...

We decide to do a little shopping before we went to the pool. We walked into one store, and as I was walking through the door, I notice the guy from last night. The one that was walking away from the table by Dev when we were walking up. This is beginning to get a little weird. It almost seems like he's wherever I am although this is only the second time I'm seeing him; I think...

He mistakenly bumped into me and said, "Excuse me." Smiled a half smile and eased past me out of the door. There's something so familiar about him. Is it his eyes? That smile is familiar too. But the long hair is why I think I don't know him. Maybe he just favors someone? Maybe we went to school together? I shrug off my thoughts. Weird. A few hours pass and Janae says she's ready to go to the pool.

We decide to head back to the hotel. We go through the lobby and through the doors to the pool area.

As we approach the pool area, the scene is so serene. There's a family of four sunbathing in the east of us and a gay couple to the west of us applying sunscreen. The pool area is unimaginable. There's a lazy river, a swim-up bar, and cabanas for days all around the pool. We find a spot to the south of us that no one seems to be interested in. There are several empty seats surrounding us under the cabana and in front of it and we love it. Seems perfect. No couples. No children. No distractions. We each realize at the same time we don't even have our swimsuits on to sunbathe. So in unison, "I need to change. Yeah, me too. Wait! What?" We start laughing hysterically. "Jinx! Double jinx!" I put one hand over my mouth, trying to silence the laughter inside of me. "You're buying me a Coke, bitch! With crown!" Janae laughs as she starts walking toward the locker rooms. I'm still dying laughing, so I don't protest.

As I follow suit, to my left I notice a guy with his sunglasses on his nose looking at me. DAMN he's fine! Shit! Where they make them at? I walk past, pretending not to see him and I hear, "PST, PST, hey!" I continue walking, sashaying away, and then I feel a firm hand on my shoulder with a person saying, "Girl, let me show you what life is. Let me show you the world. Let me make love to you for hours. Damn, girl, I want to drink your bath water!"

I stop. SHIT! I just got in a relationship yesterday! Like, fuck! Where the fuck were you a couple weeks ago? I turn around, putting my arm out to remove his hand. "Sorry, dude, I'm taken." Damn never said those words before. It made me feel good but stuck wondering if I was ready for a relationship at the same time. Like, really? We just initially started talking yesterday. Yesterday! Relationship? I mean damn, I want the dude, but damn!

"Oh, are you?" says the handsome voice, but I'm too busy looking down at his big ass light-skinned feet in them flip-flops. Damn, that's some big feet! Shiiiiiiit! Dude gotta be hung like Ron Jeremy. I shake my head and look up. Oh, chute its Dev! Ha! Glad I ain't say no crazy shit!

"Oh, shit! Hey, bae!" I say, overly excited. I swear I thought it was ol dude coming to scoop me up and take me away. I hurry and hug him. Shit. Act cool. Act cool, lil bihh! But man! When he put his arms around me and put his nose by my ear, and took a deep breath, it was all over. What dude? Who?

Now I have to pause for a minute and explain what I'm feeling. I have one hand just above my ass, the other on the back of my neck cradling my head. The hand that's near my ass slowly moves toward the top of my ass and the other is bringing my whole head closer to his face. At the present moment, he's just staring at me. But meanwhile, his hand drops to the part of my ass that meets my leg. Yep, that part. Then it sensually squeezes… Okay… Right now, it's time for him to go ahead and enter his pleasure rod into my lady garden, 'cause looking into those eyes, being in his grasp, makes me want to combust whatever may be left from the day he wasn't even there!

And then, again, it happens. He kisses me. Deeply, sensually, sexually. I ain't lying. I can't take it anymore! I stop the kiss, "My bed in fifteen?" I say searching for air.

He quickly picked me up like I'm a sandbag in one swoop, "Girl, bed now!" He turns toward the room and we hear Janae hollering after us. "Come on y'all! Not right nah! Fuuuuuuck! We were about to chill," she says, annoyed, smacking her lips. "Deeeeev!" she screams slouching in a chair. "Make sure he wears a rubber, yo!" she yells while cupping her mouth like a microphone.

We laugh, but I don't think we will have any time for that!

Chapter 8

He held me on his shoulders the whole elevator ride. There was a family in the elevator dressed as if they were in the Bahamas. Island shirts, shorts, and sandals. From around Dev, I could see the family staring at us in awe. The mother of the son covered his eyes, trying to prevent him from looking up my dress. Dev then puts his hand over my ass, but I doubt it hurt the little boy's imagination! We make it to the room in what seemed like seconds. He puts me down and we start tearing away at each other's clothes. I pull his Aeropostale shirt off. He slips the straps of my dress over my shoulders, and it falls to the floor revealing my braless breasts and red-laced Victoria secret thongs. He begins kissing me with so much authority. So much control. Like, "I'm the man" and that he is! He starts kissing me on my neck, to my earlobes, back to my lips. He has a hand full of my right breast, while his left hand is pulling and tugging at my right ass cheek. I start pushing down on his swim trucks making them fall to the floor. He steps out of them, picks me up, and carries me to my bedroom. He gently lays me on the bed and steps back to admire my body as if it were art. This is nothing like I imagined. I'm lying in a supine position, and this feels so unsexy… But I am clean shaven, so hopefully, that's a plus to some sexiness. I lift my left leg in the air, pointing my toe, opening my legs a little. I sit my left foot down on the bed and do the same with the right leg. When I put it down I leave both legs wide open. Moving my knees opposite of each other left to right like my lady garden is playing peek-a-boo. He has a front row seat to my peep show and by the looks of it, he is enjoying every single minute!

"Damn, girl, you wet!" he says, licking his lips, looking down at my sweet spot. "Slide up." He demands, motioning his hands to the head of the bed. I like this. Take control, baby. I'm at your disposal! I do as I'm told, straightening my legs as I laid my head on a pillow with my arms at my sides while waiting for more instructions. He slides from the foot of the bed on top of me like a figure skater on ice. So graceful. So dominant. He straddles me, laying his big hard pole on my stomach and leans over putting his left hand behind my head and the right on my cheek. He begins kissing me once again, making his tongue do jumping jacks against mine. Whirling and twirling we play tug of war with our tongues. He starts to move his pleasure rod up and down my stomach like he's letting me know how he's going to give it to me. Grinding slow but steady. I want it. I want it bad. I raise my hands to his fully toned chest, but he sits up grabbing both raising them above my head holding them down by my hands firmly and begins to kiss my breasts. He licks the left nipple so gently it sends tingles down my spine. He goes to the right doing the same but this time bites a little. Not too hard, but enough to make my lady garden flowers ruffle. Okay! Enough foreplay! *Let's get this party started*, I scream in my head. Almost as though he heard me he sits up then lean over pulling down on my thongs with his teeth to remove them. Once he got them to my knees, he raises up saying, "Girl, these things are soaked!" he says, smiling from ear to ear once he had completely removed them. Throwing them behind him, he grabs each leg with each hand and raises them and repositions his hands, placing them on my thighs. Spread eagle. He reaches over to the left side of the bed and grabs a rubber. When did that get there? I cover my face. Although this is what I want and have been dreaming of for forever, I am now actually embarrassed. I mean come on. Have you really looked at a vagina? It's not cute!

"Umm, Jazmynn? You uh..." letting go of my legs pointing at my lady garden with his right-hand finger and climbing out of bed. His pleasure rod is decreasing in size. NO, NO, NO, NO! What the hell? What's wrong? Do I stink? I've never had any odor down there!

EVER! I rub my hand on my lady garden and bring it up to my face and before I can sniff, I see it...

I see blood and realize. My CYCLE started.

Out of all motherfucking times of the month, this bitch wants to come today. TODAY! Right now. Couldn't it fucking wait until later on today?! Like really. Mother Nature got that much hater-aid in her? She knew what was about to happen. Hell, she could have sent the sign she sends every month! CRAMPS AND SPOTTING! Ugh! Devon is just standing there looking at me in total disbelief.

"Damn, Jazmynn! Couldn't you have told me this shit beforehand? Damn, girl! Imma fucking get blue balls!" he throws his hands up and down in frustration.

"I didn't know!" I say, knowing my face is full of embarrassment. Shit, I was embarrassed for him to look down there, he has, and I'm on my fucking cycle! I get up and run to the bathroom sobbing in tears. Why me? Why is this happening to me?! I look at myself in the mirror. It's blurry, but I see my lips are bright pink from all the face sucking we had been doing. I'm at a total loss! I really just for the life of me can't believe this. I wish I could talk to Janae. This very moment. I already know she would hug me and tell me everything is okay and life will go on, but I want her now. I want to just run and scream her name out the window. I wipe my tears. Take your shower and get dressed and go downstairs and meet her. I say to myself. Turning to the shower, I turn it on and let it run until it starts steaming up the mirror. Once in, I cry a few minutes more letting the water beat me in the face, then shower. When I come out, I notice Devon is gone. Damn! I scream inwardly shaking my head. Whelp, I guess I just ruined the chance of us being in any kind of relationship. He probably won't be able to even look at me.

I hear a knock at my door and quickly shout, "Come in!" Hell, if its room service delivering anything, hopefully, I can get them to have the maid come to change the comforter.

Janae peeks her head through the door and asked was it safe. HAHA. Very funny I say to myself. She probably already knows what happened and just want to get my side of the story. "Sure," I say, walking to the closet to find something to wear. About twenty minutes earlier, I was crying my eyes out from what had just happened, then cried because she wasn't there. Now I would just prefer to be alone and wallow in my unhappiness. Alone. "Sup?" I say breaking the silence.

"You tell me!" she says, smiling while picking up my blood-soaked underwear. "You might be needing these," she says, beginning to throw them my way. I stick my hands up to tell her to wait and stop but she jumps, dropping them back to the floor looking at her hand. "Girl! They full of blood. Are you on your cycle?!" she says and she walks toward the bathroom beginning to wash her hands. "Jazmynn, are you on your cycle or did Dev hurt you?" she asks again. I'm just standing there embarrassed once again speechless. Fuck my life!

"Yeah, I started. I'm sorry. I meant to pick them up," I say, running and grabbing them off the floor, throwing them into the trash can and heading to the bathroom to wash my hands. "Well, I would guess you didn't get any?" she says, coming out of the bathroom drying her hands. "You okay?" she asks. Almost as though she can see through my soul and already knows the answer. I began crying again. "Not really," I say in between sobs. She comes over and hugs me, saying, "It's gonna be okay. It's a fact of life. You can't control that. What did Dev say?" she asks as she pulls away with both hands on my shoulders. I turn away feeling sick to my stomach with embarrassment but reply.

"He asked me why didn't I tell him and I told him I didn't know, I guess when I ran to shower he left."

She hugs me once again, saying, "Girl, that's a part of womanhood, if he doesn't understand that then fuck him! Get dressed. Let's go sight-seeing," she says as she lets go of me, kisses me on my cheek, and goes sit on the foot of the bed.

Chapter 9

We decide our first stop would be at the Feetish Spa Parlor for a little relaxation. Lord knows I needed some stress relief. I got a wonderful back and face deluxe and Janae decided on the trifecta. From there we went to the Mob Museum, the Bootleg Canyon Flight lines, and finally to Mr. Mama's for a bite to eat. I checked my phone every few minutes or so, but still no word from Devon. Leaving out of Mr. Mama's, I see the guy who was at the pool earlier. He was getting in a taxi but happened to look back and notice me. He instead of getting into the taxi, closed the door back, and sent the taxi on its way. He smiled at me so warmly and began walking our way. Nae Nae quickly notices and nudges me in my side trying to take my attention off the guy for a minute.

"What?" I say in aggravation.

"You're taken, remember?" she says to me.

"Yeah, so? I can look, can't I?"

"Sure you can, just know this dudes been checking you out since he saw you at the pool earlier, and he's about to come up to you," she whispers and then she walks away walking into a nearby store.

"Hi, beautiful, how are you?" he asks as he reaches his hand out for a handshake. He's at least six-foot-two, dark chocolate, and two hundred pounds, easy.

"I'm fine and you?" I say, returning his handshake.

"My name is Peter. Peter Williamson, and I'm pleased to make your acquaintance. Would you by any chance like to take a stroll?"

He points down the sidewalk toward the American Campgrounds Park. "I would, but sorry, I'm in a relationship, and I don't think my boyfriend would be too fond of me taking strolls with other men while we're on vacation." I smile sweetly.

He looks at me and says, "Girl, if you were mine you wouldn't be caught alone while we're on vacation. Anyway, now that that part's out the way (referring to my relationship status) would you care to take an innocent stroll?"

"Did you not just hear what I said? I'm taken." I say, unfazed.

He is persistent! "You look single to me standing here. And yes, I heard you. I just would like to take a stroll with a lovely young woman with no strings attached. It is just a walk. If he gets mad at you for walking with a complete stranger, he's a fool."

I think about it for a moment, "Okay." I say, "But my friend Janae is coming with us," I say, turning to walk into the store she went into when she left me, but she is already exiting. She had to have been watching through the window, or this is one big fucking coincidence.

"Hey, let's walk with him to the park," I spit out.

"For what?!" exclaims Nae Nae, looking completely disinterested.

"Well," I say, inhaling deeply, "he wants to walk with me, but I don't want to go alone, so I told him you were coming with us," I answer trying to sound like I'm in control. "Damn! Why me?" Janae answers, throwing both hands up. "You can be scandalous by yourself instead of including me in your shit!" she giggled and walked over to Peter. Holding out her hand she says, "Hi, I'm Janae, Jazmynn's BEST friend. And you are?"

Peter accepts her handshake and replies chuckling, "Peter Williamson. Nice to meet you, Ms. Janae." He winks. He must've sensed the seriousness. Haha! "Are we ready to go for our walk?" he asks directly to me.

"Sure," I say but deep down, feels it's so wrong.

As we walk, we find out Peter is an entrepreneur who owns a few businesses here in Vegas and across the United States in several other states. He was initially only out here for a business meeting but later decided to make a small vacation out of the trip. He was the oldest of his four siblings, from Houston, Texas, and had no children. After sitting in the park for a while, I look at my phone to see the time and notice I have two text messages from Dev. The first one said, "I'm so sorry for leaving you like that. Please forgive me. I've never been in that situation before and didn't know how to deal with it. I now realize that wasn't the mature way to handle it and I apologize. I hope you still love me as I do you. Xoxo, Dev."

I smile to myself. How sweet. The next message says, "I'm back in the room, wy@?"

As I begin to text him back, Peter says "Your old man looking for you now, huh?"

"What?" I say with a quizzical look on my face. "Nah, just friends from back home wondering when we coming back." Okay, I lied! Janae gives me a pair of eyes. I text Dev: "Walking in the park. We'll be back shortly."

Close my phone and put it up. It vibrates almost immediately. I pull it back out and look at it, Dev: "Which one? Imma come to meet y'all."

Oh shit! I can't tell him what park I'm at because if he comes and sees this dude here I don't know what he will think. But on the other hand, dude can be passed off like he's trying to talk to Janae. What to do? What to do?

Janae notices me in deep thought and asks, "Everything okay?"

"Yeah," I say. "Just a little tired." Yeah, that's right. Just do everything possible to leave and then I can just tell Dev we are already on our way back.

Janae standing to her feet extending her hand once more to Peter. "It was nice meeting you, Pete, but I'm tired as well. We are going to head back to our room to get a little rest so we can party tonight."

"Oh! Okay cool." He stands, accepting her handshake once more, smiling, and showing the most gorgeous set of teeth. "How long are you guys in town for, and where are you guys partying at?"

"We're leaving tomorrow night, and since we don't know much about the area, we will do a little bar hopping," I answer, reaching my hand out to say goodbye, trying to cut this start of another conversation off.

"Yeah, today's her birthday," says Janae looking at her phone completely ignoring my short comment.

"Is that so?" Peter asks, raising an eyebrow. "Well, if you guys happen to end up at Hennessey's Tavern, tell them Pete sent you. I will make sure VIP is sectioned off and all drinks will be on the house and the finger food too!"

"Wow! Thanks!" Janae says, looking up from her phone, impressed.

"You don't have to…" I try to say but he immediately cuts me off. "It's no biggie. Hey, I may pop in to do a birthday toast." He winks, grabbing my left hand giving it three tiny kisses.

"Well, we aren't sure exactly how much bar hopping we will do. We may find one we like and stay there the whole night," I say, pulling my hand out of his.

"That's fine too." He smirked, replying, "The invitation will still be open if you change your mind." He salutes us, chunks up the deuces, and walks away. He got in my head and knows it. Damn. He is fine, though. Like, very fine.

Chapter 10

We arrive back at the room, and Dev is fast asleep on the couch. We decided not to wake him and go to my room to look for our outfits for the night. I told Peter I was tired earlier, which was a lie, but now, I would actually like to shower, put on some baggie clothes, and cuddle up in my bed eating snacks and watching movies. Then again, the more I think about it, the more I think about the fact it's my birthday it only comes once a year, and shit! People don't get to come to Vegas every day. I need to live this up. Hell, we leaving tomorrow. I can sleep on the way home and sleep when I get home.

Janae pulls out a gold glittery tight-fit short bodycon dress and some red heels. She then goes to my jewelry box and pulls out some red studs, a red stone anklet, and my red finger-nail polish. Call me crazy, but it's actually in there to keep it hidden from her! She loves the color, but that bottle was too expensive for her to be using every other day! I didn't think she knew where it was, now the cat's out the bag. Damn!

"What you watching me for? Go take your shower and wash that oily head of yours. You about to get a makeover boo!" says Janae with her gorgeous smile on her face.

"A makeover?" I say, half smiling because I'm confused.

"Yes, ma'am! A makeover. Now go wash your ass!" she points to the bathroom.

I grab my under clothes, tampon, and robe, and do as she says. I'm not sure if I should be excited or scared. I'm not too much of a risk taker, but tonight, I think I'll go out on a limb and give it a shot.

When I come out of the bathroom, Janae is sitting on the bed with a footstool in front of her and the blow dryer in hand. "Sit," she demands. I sit. Like a little fucking kid in one of those little plastic chairs getting their hair done by their mom. I sigh; I'm just waiting to see the outcome. She passes the brush through my damp hair and then begins to blow drying the crap out of it. Piece by piece by piece by piece as we sit in silence. Ugh! I never thought she would finish. Then she begins flat-ironing my hair taking it piece by piece making me tilt my head here and there to get hard to reach areas. She bends down to my ear and began talking low. "So we gonna go to that bar, or nah?"

"Girl, no! You know that dude trying to holla at me, how am I gonna explain to Dev we at this bar drinking free all night 'cause this dude invited us and probably wants to date me? No. Ah-ah. Nope. Ain't doing it. Not a chance," I sternly whisper.

"Girl, I got you. You won't have to worry about anything. Once Dev starts drinking, he ain't gonna know what's been paid for and what's free anyway! Come on, girl, don't be a pussy!" she whispers, giggling playfully.

"Janae! I said no, the answer is no! There are a million other bars to go to." I snapped, almost spitting fire. I don't have time for this. Dev and I literally just started dating. I don't need any bullshit to have me looking like a hoe.

"Damn! Okay. It ain't even that serious," she says, twirling the hot flat-iron by my face. We don't talk for the next four or five minutes. Maybe I pissed her off, but I don't care. She'll live. She tries to make too many of my decisions sometimes, and it annoys the shit out of me. I don't feel like having to try to deal with avoiding Peter and trying to keep shit from Dev. Starting a relationship built on lies is for the birds.

I begin to think about what happened with me and Dev earlier today and start to tear up again. Janae notices and hugs me around my neck. "I'm sorry, boo, I ain't mean to make you mad," she says while letting go and gently starting back on my hair.

"It's not you. I was just thinking about what happened earlier today. I'm still so embarrassed. I really don't think I will be even able to look Dev in the face ever again," I say as I wipe a tear from my eye. "I really, really don't think I will be able to. I feel like he's going to look at me and think of what happened and be totally disgusted. What if things get heated between us again? Hell, will things ever get heated between us again?! And if so, when I undress will he think of what happened and lose interest and make me be the reason the mood was ruined again? Ugh!" *Stop crying this instant!* I say to myself.

"Girl, everything is fine like I told you earlier, he will get over it! Guys have a short attention span. He done probably already forgot what happened. Stop crying and come on and get up so I can do your makeup before I put your curls." I stand to my feet and walk over to the chair at the vanity mirror. Pull out the chair to sit and Janae stops me.

"Hey, you know what? Go ahead and get dressed first. Imma go take my shower real quick and do your finishing touches to your hair and your makeup when I get out." She exits my room and goes into hers, grabbing underclothes and her robe. I walk to the closet, open the doors, and stand there. What the hell am I gonna wear? She got this badass dress out she's wearing and Imma look like shit next to her! I start tearing up again! Damn it! She begins to close the door to the bathroom and stops. "Bitch, you crying AGAIN?! What now?" sounding annoyed with all her stuff under her left arm and her hand on her hip.

"It's nothing," I say.

"Shit, it's gotta be something! What you crying about now?" she asks, rolling her eyes. "I know you on your cycle and emotional and shit, but damn! You need to get this shit together! You wanna stay home tonight?"

"I don't have anything to wear tonight," I say quietly. My hormones are out of whack, and it is not only annoying to me, but to her as well.

"Jazmynn, why in the hell do you think that dress is laid out on the bed with everything that's gonna go with it? Do you think it's a display? Do you think I just did all that for the hell of it 'cause I'm bored?" she says sarcastically while looking at me with eyes ablaze.

"Well, no," I say meekly, "I mean, I thought that was your stuff you were laying out for you to wear tonight," I answered, putting my head down in shame. God, I'm so stupid. Of course, it's for me. It's my birthday!

"Jazmynn. If you don't get your ass in that dress and put all that shit on, it's gonna be me and you! I bought the damn dress for you to wear tonight. Makeover. REMEMBER?" she says, hitting her forehead as if "DUH, STUPID."

"I want you to sparkle like the gem you are, stand out, and be seen by all that are near or far," she says as she points near her foot and then to the door. "That's your outfit, boo! I'm wearing a black little black dress it's on my bed if you wanna look at it." Shaking her head in aggravation she finishes with, "Let me go take my damn shower. Go put your damn clothes on!" she says, heading to her original destination.

Wow, and I lay my eyes on the bed! This dress is so gorgeous. Definitely has to be handmade. Earlier when I glanced at it, I thought it was sequins, but looking at it up close, it is tiny rhinestones. Tiny white rhinestones that glitter reflecting the gold material of the dress and the light. I'm about to be so cute! Thanks, Janae! I slip on the dress, it's kind of heavy. It's most probably because of the million beads it took to make it. I put in my studs, fasten my anklet, and put on my heels and head to the full-length mirror. I look stunning! The dress hugs every curve I have. I'm a little bloated, but it doesn't matter. It's still the bomb.com. I grab my bottle of Giorgio Armani, spray a little under my dress, behind my ears, and down my cleavage. Now all I need to do is sit and wait for Janae to come out and do my makeup and hair for tonight. Tonight. I hope this is a night to remember. It will be. I feel it in my soul.

I get back up and go turn on the radio. I make sure to not turn it too loud to wake Devon. The song "Rack City" by Tyga is playing, and I sooooooo love that song! I start singing in the full-length mirror and dancing. "Rack City bitch, rack, rack city, bitch. Ten, ten, ten twenties on ya titties, bitch!" popping my ass up and down to the beat.

Janae comes out of the bathroom dancing and singing along until the song goes off. "Whooo! That's that shit right there!" Nae Nae says, pointing at the radio. "Oh shit!" grabbing my arm, twirling me like the little dancer in a music box. "Damn, girl. Where you get all that?" pointing at my ass.

"Well, you know," I say, bowing my neck to the side with a side grin putting my arms up in the air twirling once more, "Surgery does wonders!" I start laughing. Hell, I couldn't think of anything else witty to say.

"Bitch, you stupid!" Janae says, laughing hysterically, motioning for me to come closer. We hug each other tightly. I love that girl so much. She's been better to me than my own mom. My blood.

Another good song is coming on the radio now, but Janae disconnects our embrace and says, "Imma go dress real quick. Then I can finish you and do my makeup and go. "Okay," I say back to her, dancing again in the mirror singing "Next Breath" by Tank. "As I pour this glass of wine, I hope it helps me express these thoughts of mind. (Nooo) I don't think I've ever felt the way I feel for you girl so I'm turning these lights down and telling you right now…" Sing to me Tank! "I'm sorry for the times that I stress you out. And I'm thankful for the times you ain't put me out your house…" Damn, that dude has vocals! This song is the shit! He did the damn thing! Janae comes out of her room singing along, "I don't think I've ever, ever really told you, how much I need you. I need you more than my next breath." The song finally ends and the station goes on commercial so I make my way back to the vanity so Janae can get to work.

She already has all her makeup lined up on the counter. She grabs something, turns my chair where I can only see the mirror through the corner of my left eye, and go to work. It seems like it's taking her forever! She puts something cool and wet on my face, then some kind of powder, then she draw on my eyebrows, then it feels like lipstick being smeared on my eyebrows and certain parts of my face. She takes a brush and begins brushing those same spots, and I begin to think. Do I need that much improvement? Do I have that many flaws? Damn! I'm getting ready to shed yet more tears 'cause now I feel I'm so ugly I need her to paint a pretty face on me! Janae of course notices and asks, "What's wrong?"

"Am I that ugly?" I ask, holding in tears.

"What?!" she says taking a step back from my chair. "Whachu talking about?" she asks, looking at me like I'm a child who can't correctly speak.

"You've put like twenty different products on my face and you're still going. It's been a good twenty to thirty minutes. Am I that ugly I need extra?" I ask as a tear tries to escape. The tear builds up in my right eye, and as I go to wipe it away, she slaps my hand. "Girl, you are gorgeous! All I'm trying to do is enhance your beauty. Don't you touch that eye! I done put in too much work!" I put down my head and she lifts it back to her taking a napkin and dabbing the corners of my eyes. "Lip gloss. That's all that's left is lip gloss. You can't see anything until I'm completely done, okay?" she says with authority like I'm a child.

"Okay," I say meekly, folding my arms like a child! Ugh! She slaps on my lip gloss, tells me to rub my lips and turns the chair all the way away from the mirror. "Stand up," she says, pushing the chair out so she can have room to move behind me and the vanity counter to lay the flat-iron on. I do as I'm told and then sit back down. I barely feel her in my hair this time. Almost felt like a mini head massage. I was beginning to get sooooo sleepy when she abruptly said, "All done! Now be honest and tell me the truth. If you don't like anything about your makeup or hair, let me know. I ain't tripping. I can tone it down a little more." She smiles as she spins me around back to face the vanity mirror… And oh my God! That can't be me. No way. Ah-ah! Brows on point, lashes for days, and my hair! I didn't even know it could do that! It's in big spiral curls with my layers hugging my cheeks and the longer ones falling just above my breasts. I look like a model in *Ebony* magazine! Everything looks so enhanced. My eyes have gold glitter on them, and even though I would look at the next woman and say that is too much, I feel I need more! I'm pleased. Very pleased.

"Damn, Nae Nae!" I say with excitement. "I love it!" I never noticed she had walked away while I was admiring myself in the mirror. She walked back up with her camera in hand smiling while responding, "I'm so glad you like it!" Snap! Snap! Snap! Snap! Snap! Snap! Snap! Snap! Snap! Snap! Snap! Snap! Snap! Snap! Snap! Snap! Snap!

"Okay, turn to your side and put your hand on your hip." I do so. "Yep just like that! Now move, girl! Do some poses!" she says excitedly.

I turn to my left, and back to my right. I stick my ass out a little and point at it with my left pointer. I lay on the bed, put my hand palm up on my head like I'm in distress, then get up. I go back to the vanity and sit in the chair with my legs crossed and an arch in my back. I then sit in the chair backward and look straightforward and let her get a few of my backside. I then decide to get up and stop sitting in the chair backward because the dress was starting to cut off my circulation in my legs and is too tight to be doing what I'm trying to do.

Then I hear a familiar voice…

"Dayuuuuuummmm! Shit, girl! Is it my birthday?!" Dev says, pointing to his chest excitedly, cheesing from ear to ear. "Happy birthday to me! You are gorgeous!" he exclaims. Oh, shit. Dev. I hesitate to turn around still embarrassed by the events earlier. "Turn around, beautiful. Let me check you out," Dev says eagerly. I turn around and smile avoiding eye contact while unconsciously blushing a little. He's so handsome. He always seems to do that to me. I usually hurry and walk away or pretend I haven't really heard a word he has said, and just mumble thanks, but couldn't today. Did I say how handsome he is?

"Hi, there sleepyhead," I say teasingly with a half-smile. He is already dressed for tonight and I don't know how! Maybe the music was loud and that's why I hadn't heard him stirring. I don't know. Anyway, he is dressed to impress. A white tee with a black Jordan logo, dark stonewashed jeans, and some white Jordan's. He is clean-shaven and looks to have somehow gotten a haircut. Wow, he's hot.

Janae surprisingly didn't take as long on her face as she usually does, was already standing from the vanity chair spritzing perfume.

"You guys ready to party?" asked Dev.

"Hell yeah!" Janae and I say in unison before she held up a finger telling us to hold it, "Wait before we go…" she says briskly, walking to her room to grab a big bottle of alcohol she somehow had hidden and some Vegas shot cups. "We have to take a shot!" Janae says, placing the cups on the vanity opening the bottle. This girl has a whole fifth of crown royal! Damn! How many shots she wants to take? Hell, I won't make it out of the hotel room if I drink too much of that! She hands us each a cup, saying to me, "This is your birthday shot cup. It's coming with us tonight. We need to fill this cup at least twenty-six times. So here's cup number 1!" I take the cup already feeling dizzy. They are going to have to carry me back to the room drinking twenty-six shots!

Dev toasts. "Here ye, here ye! Tonight we are together to celebrate one more year of life with our beautiful best friend, my girl"—he winks and blows a kiss—"I wish you a night of fun, better yet a night to remember, and many more years of life, and the best twenty-sixth birthday ever!"

"Here, here!" we say in unison, clink our cups, and down our shot. Janae turns to the vanity and grabs the bottle of crown once more. "Cups," she says, holding the bottle up ready to pour another shot. She took in a deep breath, "Okay so, it's your twenty-sixth birthday, what do I say, what do I say? Okay, okay, I got it," she says while twirling her hair. "Jazmynn, you are my best friend, well, honestly, the sister I never had, and I appreciate your loyalty and your friendship. You've just graduated and Lord knows I hope you find a job close to home because I won't be able to make it without you! I intend on making sure you have the best night ever and I wish you many more years of life. Love you. Now let's turn the fuck up!" We clink cups once more and kill our shots. I'm so excited to see what this night will bring!

Chapter 11

We start at the bar downstairs of the hotel. Drink about four shots and decide to move on down the block. We walk in one bar that had country music blasting and walk right on out. Didn't even get a drink. Some country music is okay, but that honky tonk crap? Nah-uh. Gotta go. We hop on to the next bar; it was full of old people listening and dancing to swing out. I felt a little overdressed, but, Dev and I still danced to a couple songs. I felt like I was leaving Janae out so I grabbed her and danced with her for a few minutes as well.

"I'm having a blast going from bar to bar! Let's go to the next!" I yell over the music to Janae. She nods her head yes and signs with her hand "okay" and grabs my hand leading me off the dance floor and out the door.

We come upon a bar that looked high-class. The people who were standing in line wore fancy little black dresses, starched down jeans or suits. The valet looked very busy tonight. Soon as a car pulled up they were running opening doors, letting the people out of their vehicles and jumping in the driver seat going park the cars. From outside, you can't see anything inside because the windows are blacked out. You can't even hear any music! What kind of bar is this?! Security is at the door and asks what our names are. Janae immediately says, "Janae Christian Carter, Devon Edward Thomas, and Jazmynn Olivia Barkley." For what reason did she feel the need to give our whole names? She must be drunk! Security guy looks at his list and says "Sorry, you guys are not on here. I'm going to have to ask you guys to leave…"

"Oh well! On to the next one!" I say, unbothered, throwing my right hand in the air. It's my birthday. I don't need this bar, there are several more up the road…

Janae whirled around telling me to hold up and turned back motioning for the security guy to come closer. She inched closer and she whispers something in his ear while pointing to me.

He smiles and turns away saying something in a walkie-talkie, seconds later turns back and says, "Ladies and gentlemen, I apologize for the mix up, please come in, the hostess will show you to your private seating." He then ushers us in the door, looking scared as if he was in trouble but quickly forgetting that trouble when I passed by because of the angry onlookers that started fussing about the fact that they stood in line over an hour and still haven't been let in.

We walk in and a hostess is standing there with a tray holding champagne. CHAMPAGNE! We each take a glass and a gentleman (dressed in a black suit that looks extremely expensive) walks up behind us telling us to come this way. We follow him down a hall and finally start hearing the booming of music as we approach another door. He opens the door ushering us in. There's party lights flashing bright, a huge bar in the center of the floor, and a DJ straight ahead on a balcony with huge earphones playing "I'm Sexy and I Know It" by LMFAO. The balcony wraps around the whole bar, but it looks like more people are on the ground floor than in the balcony. The guy brings us to an elevator and selects the button VIP suite. VIP. VIP?! VIP?! I say angrily to myself now breathing fire! Damn! This is not going to be good and Janae knows this! The DJ says over the speaker as the song comes to an end, "Welcome to Hennessey's Tavern, ladies and gents, out there! All requests are welcome and played. Hope everyone has a night to remember tonight. Don't forget to tip your waiter!" Everybody screams "yeahhh" and all kinds of gibberish.

We get to the VIP floor and are brought to a cabana-like room that overlooks the whole club. The guy asks what bottles we would like, and Dev rubbing his hands together says, "Do you mean what we want to drink? Bottles? Man, we bar hopping, we don't plan on staying that long!" he says as he crosses his arms across his chest. The guy replies, "All drinks are on the house, Mr. Thomas. Compliments of Mr. Willaimson," he answers back, looking at Dev then on the floor. Dev begins to look puzzled then cups his ear in toward the guy with his left hand. "Come again, who?!" asks Dev.

Janae quickly inserts herself between the two. "We will have crown, Grey Goose, and Coke with ice please."

"Very well, Ms. Carter," he says, winking at her. She smiles sweetly back toying at a lock of hair. I think they like each other.

Dev asks Janae while jamming his hands in his front pockets, "What was that all about? Why are the drinks on the house?" he asks with a clueless look on his face.

"This club is owned by a guy I just met," she said, giving a dismissive wave of her hand as she turned to sit down on the leather couch. And that was it. She told the truth, even though it wasn't the whole truth, there were no more questions. He accepted her reply and leaned over the balcony looking down at the crowd. I sit next to Janae giving her the evil eye. As she mouths back, "I'm sorry" with a weak smile bowing her head. I ran my hand through my hair and tossed my hair at her, like whatever. I got a buzz. I took in a sharp breath. It's cool. Everything will be all right. It's my birthday, and as long as Mr. Peter doesn't come to introduce himself personally to Devon everything should be fine. I exhale. I don't want any kind of drama or confusion.

The guy makes it back with our alcohol, a bucket of ice, and cans of Coke.

Janae attempts to tip him, but he declines. She gave a half shrug and nodded, "Okay" and began opening the bottle of Grey Goose.

"Time for shots!" she yells, pumping the bottle in the air. I quickly stuck my shot cup out. Imma need to have a couple more drinks in case the shit does hit the fan! I take one shot then stick my cup out for another. I know I'm fucking up mixing brown with clear, but at this moment, I really don't give a fuck. I grab a glass, put some ice in it, pour half a glass of crown and filled up the rest with Coke. A fast song I've never heard comes on and I jump up to dance grabbing Janae on the way up. We throw one hand in the air holding our drinks in the other and bounce our ass to the beat. Dev comes up behind me and pulls my waist to his, moving when I move. The song finally ends and we sit to take a break. A hostess comes placing a tray of turkey sandwiches and a tray of wings with ranch and barbecue sauce. Then leaves.

She quickly returns with a vegetable tray and a fruit tray. Leaving again only to return with several bottles of water and napkins. As she placed them on the table in front of us she yells over the music asking if we need anything else. We shake our heads no in unison. We are all in shock. She looks as if she doesn't even notice our expressions. She mouths okay then picks up the wrappers from the alcohol bottles and the empty can of Coke and attempts to leave, as Janae stands and stops her. She leans over and whispers in her ear and offers to tip her, but the waiter held her finger up and mouthed, "I'm sorry, ma'am, I cannot accept your tip."

She then turns and steps out of sight. I've already finished my drink so I fix another and stand to my feet again dancing. I look toward the entrance of our VIP and notice a guy in a suit standing blocking it with red rope. Do we have security? Whaaaat! That's what's up! I look over the balcony and at the same time, a spotlight shines on me with the most blinding light. The whole club goes dark besides the light that shines on me, and what looks like a lamp by the DJ. I put my left hand over my eyes like a visor trying to look and see what was going on while placing my drink down and resting my right hand on my hip. The music is turned to a hum and the DJ begins to speak. "Ladies and gentlemen, please turn your attention to the VIP executive suite to your top left. We have the beautiful Ms. Jazmynn here celebrating her twenty-sixth birthday. Please raise your glasses, shots, or bottled water, but if you have bottled water, you really should leave! HAHA! But hey, let's toast to her. Ms. Jazmynn, we at Hennessey's Tavern wish you a wonderful birthday with many years to come, and if there is anything else we can do to make your night memorable, please don't hesitate to ask! Happy birthday, gorgeous, this song is for you."

"It's your birthday so I know you want to ride out. Even if we only go to my house. Sip mo-eezy as we sit upon my couch. Feels good, but I know you want to cry out…" I smile and wave to the people below. The lights are turned back on party mode, and I throw my drink in the air as though I'm toasting back to them and down it. Everyone screams happy birthday and start chanting, "Come down!" I look at Janae and Dev to see if they want to go. Dev looking all warm and cozy like he's getting drunk says, "Go on, girl. Enjoy yourself. Imma make that birthday sex up to you when you… you know." He laughs. Janae says "Come on girl before the song ends!" grabbing my hand dragging me to some stairs down to the bottom floor I had never seen. The spotlight follows my every step. The light reflects off my dress making me look like I'm wearing diamonds. Once on the floor, people make a walkway for me until I get to the center of the dance floor. I start dancing winding my ass clockwise to the beat. "Girl, you know I-I-I, girl you know I-I-I. I been fiending. Wake up in the late night. Been dreaming about your loving, girl…"

Peter comes up to me, kisses me on the cheek, and hands me a drink. I give him my empty glass winding and grinding away. We dance to two fast songs and one country one. I need a breather, but before I can leave the dance floor; a group of chicks push people back and make some kind of soul train line telling me it's my turn. I sashay over, winding and popping my ass a little bit and as the song ends, bend over touching my toes slowly standing up while dragging my hands up my legs, to my thighs. I pass them over my ass and pat it making the crowd go crazy. Janae and I dance a few more songs and I'm ready to go back to VIP. "I'm having too much fun down here, meet you in a few," yells Janae over the music. I pout, but she turns around talking to some new found friends. Isn't it amazing how many friends girls make when they're in a club drinking? Next morning, you don't even remember their name!

I go back up the stairs, staggering a little. I bump into a guy and tell him "Excuse me, I think I'm drunk." Then I stop. "I know you!" I say, pointing my drunk index finger in his face.

"I'm sorry, but no you don't," he answers. I stare at him for a moment. He has a beard and a mustache with a head full of curly hair and gorgeous green eyes. I can't shake how familiar he looks and how those eyes remind me so much of Dev. I continue on my journey back to VIP. I need to eat something, I'm so glad that the hostess brought sandwiches. I grab one and sit on the couch munching away. Where's Dev, I wonder, looking across Henny's tavern…

I finish my couple sandwiches, fix me another drink, and go back down to the dance floor and meet Janae. She is now talking to a cute guy who she introduced to me as Steven the college professor. He looks to me like a high school dropout, but who knows? In the club, you can be whoever you want to be. Janae asked him if he was going to buy her a drink. (She's so forward. No beating around the bush!) I don't know what his answer was exactly, but it must've been no. All I know is she told him to fuck off, she's drinking for free all night anyway because she's VIP. And he salutes and walks away.

I throw up the peace sign. Bye, Professor Steven! Haha! A song comes on, and Janae and I make some random guy a sandwich between us dancing away. She's in the front of him, and I'm bumping my ass against his. Poor thing, he has no moves. Hope he's not that stiff in bed. Janae would walk out. She has no shame in her game. Thinking about a bed. It's almost 2:00 a.m., and the activities of the day are finally catching up to me. I'm still drinking, but getting tired as hell! My mind begins to wonder where Dev is again. I haven't seen him for most of the night. Hell, I haven't gotten but one dance with him. I decide to go back to the balcony and stay there in case he comes back up there if he's down here. I figure if he sees me sitting alone, he will come to keep me company, or at least ask if something is wrong. I sit. And wait, and wait, and wait. No Devon! Where could he be?

I decided to ask our security if he saw where he went, and he said toward the restroom about an hour ago. Damn! Is he asleep on the toilet?! He was toasted before my birthday dance if he kept drinking he's so done! I asked if there was a way he could have someone check the restroom for him for me, just to make sure he was okay. If he's still in there that is.

Chapter 12

HOME SWEET HOME! Back to reality. As I unpack, I recall all the events from the past week. So much has happened. Devon is still in jail and has to stay until his court date, which he doesn't know yet. All we just know is that he doesn't have a bond. I really can't believe this shit. Our last day consisted of being questioned by a police officer after police officer about some shit we knew nothing about until lights came on in the club, and everyone being asked to exit, EXCEPT THE VIP EXECUTIVE SUITE. Janae was on the floor dancing and flew up to the balcony to my side. "Are you okay? There are cops all over down there! This doesn't seem like a club someone would shoot in or anything. Wouldn't be able to hear the shots anyway," Janae says, looking over the balcony. "Where's Dev?" Janae asks, turning back to me.

"Hell, I don't know! I haven't seen him for a good while! I thought he went down to mingle or look for us. Hell, I haven't seen him since my birthday dance! I asked the security guy to check the restroom because he said he saw Dev walk that way, but I don't know yet. He hasn't told me anything," I say becoming alarmed. We both scan the crowd with our eyes for Dev while watching as police officers are getting everyone's photo id. Viewing it, then giving it back to them and letting them leave the building. We go to walk past the security guy that was standing guarding the entrance, and he tells us we can't leave. That he has orders to keep us where we are until our third party is found. Janae flips her lid. "Bullshit! Like hell, we have to stay up here not knowing what the fuck is going on, and all the other people down there get to leave! Move the fuck out of my way! Shit!" she attempts to push past him but doesn't budge him an inch.

"Ma'am, I apologize for your inconvenience, but, I do have to do my job and keep you right here. It would be so much easier if you comply," says the guard. "Why do we have to stay here, huh? What did we do?" asked Janae.

"Ma'am, from my understanding, you guys have not done anything, it is the guy that was with you."

"What do you mean? What's going on?! What happened?" Janae concernedly asks. "I'm not obligated to disclose any information of the investigation, but an officer should be here to talk to the two of you shortly."

He turns around before Janae could ask another question. Janae turns to me. "I'm so lost! What the hell is going on?"

"I'm lost too! Dev has been gone from up here for a while. We were all having a blast dancing and shit. I just figured he made some friends and was partying like us!" Hell, I truthfully forgot we were in a relationship on that dance floor. Shit, it's been forever since I was in one! He might've gone back to the room mad!

An officer walks past our guard to us and extends his hand to me. "Good morning, ladies, I'm officer Baraco," changing hands to Janae's. "I need to ask you two ladies a few questions about the events tonight. Ahm. What are your names?" He's looking at me, I guess I go first. "Jazmynn Barkley," I say shortly and Janae answers, "Janae Carter."

"Okay, ladies, I will ask a series of questions. It won't take long if you please cooperate. I do want to let the both of you know you have the right to remain silent. Anything you say can and will be used against you in the court of law. You have the right to an attorney. If you can't afford one, the courts will provide one free of charge. Do you understand your rights?"

"Yes," we say in unison.

"So, are we being detained?" Asked Janae nonchalantly.

"Okay." Officer Baraco clears his throat and ignores her question. "Ms. Janae, you came in last night with Ms. Jazmynn, correct?"

"Yes," she answers, looking at me like she's scared. I walk to her side and grab her left hand in mine. I see the couch behind us so I tug her hand to sit. We sit. She sighs then grabs her hand from my grip and places it with her other on her lap. This time Janae clears her throat.

"Officer, before you completely begin, I have a couple questions for you. What is going on, are we suspects, and do we need a lawyer? ARE WE UNDER ARREST?!"

"Well, ma'am. It is always your right to have a lawyer, which is why I read you your rights, and if that is something you prefer, you should call your lawyer and we will continue this investigation at the prescient…"

"You did not answer my question. Are we suspects? Are we being detained? And what's going on?" says Janae getting frustrated.

"What time did you arrive?" Officer Baraco asks, completely ignoring Janae's question again.

"What?" Janae answers with a puzzled look on her face. "Are you really going to just avoid my question like that? Seriously?!" she says as though she's about to break down. She takes in a deep breath and sighs shrugging her shoulders. "I don't know," she answers, sounding defeated. Baraco clears his throat as he looks sympathetically at us and says, "The owner of this fine establishment was beaten in the restroom. This looks to be a possible case of attempted murder. The two of you are being questioned to be sure you weren't accessories to the fact. Now, may I continue with my questions, or would you ladies rather your lawyer and I bring you guys to the prescient?" Janae looks at me then back to Officer Baraco. "We don't have anything to hide. Do we, Jazmynn?"

I shake my head no. I still don't understand what the hell this has to do with us though? We can't go in the men's restroom anyway! But this shit is crazy! Somebody beat Peter and left him for dead? Do they think its Dev?!

"Go on. Ask your questions." She rushes him. She's tired. Hell, we both are. It's a little past 3:00 a.m. We have been partying since yesterday evening!

"Who is the guy that you girls came in with tonight?" asked Baraco.

"He's my boyfriend and a good friend of Janae's," I answer. "By the way, he's missing. We have been looking for him…" He starts scribbling on his notepad.

"Looking for him? For how long?" asks Officer Baraco.

"I don't know!" I snap. "Since the officers shut the club down I guess."

"Do you guys know the owner of this bar?" asks Baraco.

"Yes," we answer in unison.

"How do you girls know the owner of this bar?" he asks.

"We met him earlier today in a park," replied Janae. "What does this have to do with us?"

"Well, we are led to believe your friend is the suspect who attacked the owner in the restroom," says Baraco, studying our reactions. Is this cop serious? Devon wouldn't hurt a fly! Hell Devon doesn't even know Peter! "Devon doesn't even know Peter. He wasn't even with us when we met Peter in the park today. He was in the room sleep," I say in defense of Devon.

"But it was indeed you who asked the security to go check the restroom, was it not?" Cutting my eyes at him. Damn bastard! I had nothing to do with nothing! "Yeah," I say, putting my head down in defeat.

Baraco said, "So question, Ms. Jazmynn. You say you and this Devon guy are in a relationship?"

"Yes," I hiss.

Baraco said, "Several people saw Mr. Williamson kiss you on the dance floor, were you two having some sort of an affair?" Janae jumped to her feet. "How dare you insinuate…"

"Sit down, Ms. Carter!" he said in a stern voice.

"I will not!" screamed Janae. She was livid. She starts pacing the floor running her left hand through her hair and bringing it to her chin as though in deep thought.

Baraco says to Janae, "Have a seat, please."

She glares daggers at him then she sits. Crosses her arms and clinch her teeth.

"Do either of you ladies know where the suspect is?" asks Baraco.

Standing to her feet once again, "If I did, I wouldn't fucking tell you!" she says pointing at him. He twitches. It seems his whole demeanor changes. I think he's had enough of her outbursts.

I hold my hand out to her reaching for hers urging her to sit while officer Baraco is now reaching on his side to pull out his handcuffs. "Ladies, I will need to take the both of you in to continue this investigation." Looking at Janae and holding both hands out. "We can do this the easy way." He shows the empty hand. "Or the hard way." Showing the hand with the cuffs.

"We've cooperated and answered every single question you've asked. Why are we being arrested?" I ask on the verge of tears.

Baraco answered, "Because I have reason to believe the both of you aren't being completely honest with me." He grabs Janae's right arm and my left, then he handcuffs us together!

At the station we are separated and questioned until the police chief said it was enough, they had all they needed and sends us home. He said they viewed the video cameras that were in the club, interviewed several people that were there last night, and we were seen on the dance floor the entire time Peter was assaulted. He apologized for any confusion, our extended stay, and released us.

Eight in the morning. Eight in the fucking morning! We get back to our room, showered, and went straight to sleep. Hell, we didn't even talk about the six-hour police questioning. Nor did we during the plane ride. NOTHING! I guess we were both just too damn tired.

I slide my suitcases under my bed and flop down on the bed. Aaahhh. Before I know it, I'm out like a light.

I wake up to the aroma of breakfast. Bacon, eggs, biscuits. Shit, I'm hungry! I roll out of bed, grab underclothes, and a T-shirt and shorts, and head to the shower. I take a ten-minute shower, dress, and go to the kitchen. The smell of breakfast has filled the whole house, and the spread Janae has laid out looks like mountains of gold. I am famished!

"Good morning, love," I say.

"Morning, boo. You hungry?" she asks.

"Starved!" I say, looking at the goldmine of platters of food.

"Go on, dig in," she says, washing her last pot and handing me a plate. Ring, ring!

The house phone rings, and we both look at each other startled before either of us move to answer it. Ring, ring! It has to be Dev. He's the only person who calls the house phone unless it's a bill collector telling us we are late. I put my plate down on the counter and walk over to the phone. Ring, ring!

"He-hello?" I answer.

"Good morning. This is Cynthia Weaver with Dillard University. May I please have a word with Jazmynn Barkley?"

"This is she," I answer with a lump in my throat. This is the call I've been waiting for!

Cynthia continues, "Great, Ms. Barkley, we have recently reviewed your application and would like to schedule an interview with you for Wednesday morning at 8:00 a.m. Are you still interested in the position?"

"Is this for the counseling position?" I ask.

"Yes," she replies.

"Oh, yes, ma'am. I am very interested!" I say excitedly. I put in applications a couple days before graduation to several schools, and several to this school, but this was the one I really wanted in hopes of not having to relocate. This is perfect! Long as I land the job that is…"

"Well, Ms. Jazmynn, we will see you on Wednesday at 8:00 a.m. sharp! Hope you have a great day!" click. She hangs up before I can even tell her likewise. Janae is looking at me patiently waiting. I smile at her, grab my plate, and start fixing my breakfast.

"Okay, soooo you're just not going to tell me what that was all about?" She looks on with suspense.

"Well," I say, "I have a job interview at Dillard Stay University at 8:00 a.m. Wednesday morning. No biggie," I say, mumbling Dillard State hoping she couldn't catch it.

"Where?!" she asks, squinting her eyes at me puzzled.

I take a deep breath. Exhale slowly. I see the suspense building in her eyes. "Dillard State University!" I yell.

She jumps up with a huge smile on her face letting out a screech "Girl! That's great! It's right down the road too. So you don't necessarily have to move! I mean our living arrangement here works great, right? Oh my God! I am so happy for you! Congratulations!" She comes over, hugging me making me drop my pancake. "Let's not get beside ourselves," I say, picking it up and throwing in the trashcan. "It's just an interview. Let me get the job first!" I'm inwardly ecstatic! I hope I don't get nervous and fuck shit up. No, no, no. I will do great! I know it.

Ring! Ring! I fly to the phone this time. I don't know why. Maybe the good news who knows...

"Hello?" I answer. "This is Jazmynn."

An automated voice comes over the phone. "This is a collect call from the Southern Desert Correctional institution. Devon is requesting a call. Do you accept all charges? Press 1 for yes and 2 for no, or you may hang up and disconnect this call." Oh my God! Dev! I quickly press 1.

"Jazmynn?" I hear the sadness in his voice over the phone. "Yes, Dev. How are you?" I ask sympathetically. "Are you okay? What the hell happened?" I spit the questions out left and right.

"Look," he says, "I only have two minutes for this phone call. I will explain everything when I get home. It's not what you think. But I wanted to let y'all know they are letting me go in a few, they have to finish up some paperwork and I will be home in a few hours."

"They're letting you go? What did they say?" I ask.

"The guy was able to answer a couple questions on the way to the hospital. He didn't want to press charges, and the DA said they weren't going to press any, so I can come home. See y'all in..." and the line cuts off saying we will be charged a 39.99-dollar fee for the call.

"Well, Dev will be home in a few hours he said," I say to Janae who is now reading the newspaper.

"Oh yeah?" she asks, raising an eyebrow.

"Yeah. He said it's not what we think and he will explain more when he gets home. Girl, he said that Peter didn't press charges nor the DA," I say in amazement.

"Well," Janae looks at me concernedly. "You might want to read this. The whole incident made national news!" she says as she hands me the paper looking skeptical.

WELL-KNOWN ENTREPRENEUR BEATEN IN HIS BAR NEARLY LOSES LIFE!

> Peter Williamson, twenty-six, of Houston, Texas is currently in the intensive care unit of the North Vista Hospital in Las Vegas, Nevada. After allegedly being severely beaten by one of his customers, a Caucasian male by the name of Devon Edward Thomas, twenty-two, of New Orleans, Louisiana. Sources say Thomas allegedly attacked Williamson for unknown reasons in the restroom of his bar before fleeing the scene. Thomas was captured two blocks away and is currently being detained at the Southern Desert Correctional institution with no bond. Thomas is facing charges of attempted manslaughter. The investigation is still ongoing. The condition of Williamson has not been disclosed, but his family asks for prayers through this horrific time for a speedy recovery.

Oh my God! OH MY GOD! Attempted manslaughter! Like he tried to kill him? What in the total fuck? I probably shouldn't, but I need to send flowers. I have to do something! Dev wouldn't have been there if it wasn't for me. It's the least I can do. I can't wait until Dev gets here to explain this shit to me. I'm so lost. I stand there deep in thought, and Nae Nae breaks my concentration. "You all right, baby girl?" she asks.

Uh, no! Duh! Who would be with a situation like this?! "I guess. I mean, I'm trying to be. Dev needs to hurry and get home to explain this shit to me." I jump to my feet. "Do you think we should send flowers? I mean I know he's a guy, but considering the circumstance…" I ask Janae as I bite my bottom lip. "Yeah, it won't hurt. I will order them. Finish your breakfast," she answers. But hell, I can't! I'm not even hungry anymore.

Nae Nae is on the phone ordering flowers, and I'm still standing here stuck and in shock. I come back to earth to hear her saying, "Yes, all it needs to say is get well soon. Yes. Well, I'm not sure what room he's in, but I would guess they would get it to him if it's delivered at the hospital 'cause he's well known. Yes, that's the name I said. Oh, really? Oh, okay. Well, thanks. You too." She hangs up.

"Okay, all done," she says, walking back to the table. "At first they wanted to know what name I wanted on the card, and I was like, all it needs to say is get well soon. He doesn't need to know! Haha! He would probably send it back if he did." She laughs. "But anyway, it should get to him and I will get a text message when it arrives and is signed for," she says, sipping her orange juice.

I just don't know. I definitely won't be able to tell Dev we sent them, 'cause who knows what the exact situation is between the two or what he may think was between us two! I finish picking at my breakfast and scrape the rest in the trash and walk over to the sink and wash my dish. "What are we going to do with all these leftovers?" I ask Nae Nae. I don't know why she always cooks so much food.

"I'll fix a couple plates and walk them down to Charlie," she says, getting up and going to the cabinet for paper plates. Charlie is the neighborhood bum. He has no job, house, or car. But somehow maintains a good 350 pounds. It's probably because she feeds him daily. He never really seems to be hungry, but accepts all donations of food, clothes, and etc. He's a really sweet guy and would give the shirt off his back to anyone. Even if that's the only shirt he has. At least that's what it seems like because with all the clothes people give, he always has the same clothes on.

Nae Nae finishes fixing the food and slips on her slippers and head out of the door. Sigh. Home alone.

Chapter 13

A few hours pass and then there's a knock at the door. I rush off the couch to open the door in hopes of it finally being Dev. And it was! I throw myself into his arms hugging him tight and without delay, he begins kissing me. Better than any time before. So sensual and full of lust. At least this time if it leads to sex, I'm not on my cycle! He pushes me and moves inside using a free hand to close the door behind him. He picks me up and sits me on the counter, never disconnecting his lips from mine. He pulls me back down and during all the heavy petting we bump into the wall, then into a chair, spiraling to the couch. He raises my shirt and grabs a handful of my left breast, but I stop him. We can't do this here. I don't want Janae walking in on us.

"What's wrong? Awe, don't tell me you're on your cycle…" He pulls back to look me in my face.

"No, but we aren't doing this in here. Not here," I say, quietly pleading with my eyes.

He sighs like he's annoyed, and with one quick swoop, he picks me up, causing me to hold on with my arms around his neck and my legs around his waist, and carried me to the room.

He gently laid me on the bed, caressing me rubbing my thighs with both hands. He took a pillow and laid it across my face and told me, "Don't peek." I feel him unbuttoning my sandals, slowly slipping them off. He then kisses each toe. I don't really know how to feel about this. It's sort of freaky. I can't really say I like it, but then again I can't really say I don't. I feel him move up in the bed and stop. He gets out of bed, "Don't move or peek," he says sternly. I honestly don't know how to feel about this. Like, who the fuck he thinks he is? What the hell is he doing? But then again, I love the control. I'm having so many mixed emotions at the moment, I do what I'm told and don't move an inch. CLICK! What the hell was that? A camera?

"What was that?" I asked from under the pillow.

"Okay, I'm back!" I hear. I begin to feel him unbuttoning my jeans and attempting to pull them down at my waist so I raise my waist to help them slide down easier. They do, and in no time, he has pulled them completely off.

"Sit up and close your eyes," he demands. I pull the pillow off and squint my eyes just to take a peek. "Close them," he demands in a deeper voice. And I do submissively. He pulls off my muscle shirt and unfastens my bra and gently shoves my shoulders back to the bed replacing the pillow, this time leaving my lips from under the pillow. He then begins to kiss my left breast and then to my right. My bottom jaw drops with a light gasp, and he leans higher, beginning to tongue the hell out of me. He has my right breast cupped in his hand and is using his index finger to rub in a circular motion, causing my lady garden to flutter. He stops kissing my lips to kiss my left nipple, never stopping the beat of the circular motion of my right. His hand slides down to my panties and rubs up and down, thumbing the insertion area. I lift both legs bending at the knee to give him better access. He removes his hand but with only his fingertips, slides his fingers from my inner thigh to my right breast, circulating the cup of my breast before teasing the nipple. I'm so ready for this I can't take anymore. I raise my left arm to his chest and finally find an arm and pull it toward me. He leans in and kisses me deeply again before placing one finger on my lips and getting up moving to the foot of the bed. I feel both hands on my thighs and a warm breeze blowing through my lady garden. Then I feel soft sweet kisses between my thighs. Left to right and right to left, each time closer and closer to my sweet spot. He begins to kiss right above my panties, then a little lower and a little lower. I thrust my hips a little, letting him know I'm ready. I'm beyond ready. Enough of the foreplay. I want it. I want it bad. He giggles and I feel both hands on each side of my hips. I lift prematurely. "Slow down, baby. We got all night," he says. But he doesn't understand. A person can only take so much!

He finally takes off my panties and gently rubs my inner thighs with both hands and lifts them up at the knees. SPREAD EAGLE once again. But for real this time. He slides between my legs and rests the bend of my knees on his shoulders. He kisses my inner left thigh with short pecks. He goes up to my knee back down to my lady garden. Switching legs, he does the same. He breathes warm air on my sweet spot but never actually touches it. I'm hoping he gets to it because the intensity is overwhelming! My stomach starts to bubble. What the hell? He stops and I feel him look up at me. Lord, please don't let me have to pass gas!

Ring, ring! The house phone begins to ring. I pick my right hand up to remove the pillow and he puts it gently back down. Ring, ring!

Hell, if he's not about to do something soon I might as well answer it! Ring, ring! He then begins to slowly lick my sweet spot and I sigh 'cause FINALLY! Then my stomach bubbles once more... Ring, ring! And before I know it, my reflexes have made me pull the pillow off with my left hand and sit up with my right. Out of his grasp, out of the bed, and standing on my two feet.

"It may be important!" I say, running to the bathroom cordless phone. Phew! Safe! I release the built-up gas...

"Hello?" I say sort of out of breath. Nothing. "Hellooo?" then I hear a click as though the person hung up. Oh well! I say to myself. I start the shower and waltz back to the room. Dev is sitting on the bed looking upset. Actually looking angry. Oops! I mean, I'm sorry, but it would have been a complete turn off if I would've passed gas with him down there, you know?

"I'm sorry, Dev," I say as sweetly as I possibly can. "Let's finish this in the shower?" I say, asking more than telling.

"How?" he asks as if he's irritated. "How do I finish what I was doing in the shower?" he asks this time sarcastically.

"Well, I thought maybe we could speed up the process and move on to the next phase?" I say, walking toward him butt-ass naked.

I stand in front of him grab his left hand and place it on my left ass cheek. I grab the right and do the same. He, of course, leaves them there. I then pull his head to my breast and run my fingers through his hair then lift up his head and kiss him on the forehead. I then take a small step back and grab his left hand and tugged a little sort of asking him to stand. He does. Good boy. I turn and pull his hand leading him to the shower…

We have had hot, sticky, steamy sex at least two to three times a day and his body still yearns for more. Some days it's boring as hell, others it's like it's the first time ever. It's just not consistent. Which is annoying…

Chapter
14

Each day that passes I think more and more about Peter and wonder what exactly happened that night between him and Dev. Sitting across from Dev at the table eating dinner, I finally decide to shoot out my questions.

"Dev, what happened with that bar owner and you in the restroom? Did you try to kill him?" I ask, chewing a piece of fried pork chop.

"Well," Dev says with a mouth full of food, like he did it on purpose to avoid the question, as he has been doing every time I've asked since he got home. But not tonight! I am not about to give in and let it go. He will answer my questions, TONIGHT! I completely understand it is a hard conversation for him being he went to jail, but I deserve answers. I was there and went through trauma too!

"Well, what, Dev?" I say, irritated, remembering how aggravating and annoying the questioning I went through was.

"Well," he says wiping his mouth with his napkin, "I went to the restroom to take a piss. When I walked in he started saying how it was his club and he was allowing me to be in VIP 'cause of you and how you deserved better. I told him he didn't know me like that to be talking shit to me, and he told me he knew me because I was like every other poor Joe. That I had a good woman but couldn't do shit for her like he could. He told me I wasn't shit and would never be able to do shit for you. That I didn't deserve you. I went to leave out of the restroom 'cause he was pissing me off. *Who the fuck is this dude with this bullshit?* is what I was thinking. Then next thing I know he hit me from behind. I still tried to walk away from him but he kept instigating telling me I had been drinking on him all night that I was a bum. Then he swung again. With all those insults and with him swinging on me, I had to protect myself, Jazmynn. I didn't know him and he didn't know me, but he just wouldn't quit. I blacked out. Next thing I knew the cops were arresting me and I didn't even know how I had gotten where I was or what had happened," he says.

"I just don't understand," I say. "For what reason would he just pick a fight with you?" I say confused.

"I don't fucking know, Jazmynn, but I tell you this much. If I initiated the fight, he would've never dropped the charges. He dropped them because he knew he started it," Dev says, standing, raking his plate into the trash and throwing his plate into the sink.

"Honestly, the whole situation pisses me off, because didn't Janae say she was the one who met him and he invited her to his bar? For some reason, he sure knew your name… I was drunk, but I wasn't that fucking drunk. I remember what Janae said."

"I'm going out for a few. Don't wait up," I say, kissing his forehead and heading out the door. I'm still puzzled. I really don't see Peter as the type to start drama when he can have any woman in the world he wants. But then again, Dev doesn't know Peter so why would he? I'm getting a headache, but I really need to get to the bottom of this. I got Janae to get Peter's phone number for me a few days ago so I decided to text him. "Hi, Peter, this is Jazmynn. How are you?"

I head to Starbucks, grab a coffee, and take a seat in a back booth to not be disturbed. He doesn't text back. Maybe he's busy. Or maybe it's the wrong number. I sit for an hour or so then head home.

Back in my room, I turn the radio on and grab an ebony magazine and lay across my bed. Flipping through the pages, I see this hot guy labeled as firefighter of the month dressed in uniform. Dude sexy as hell. Dark chocolate, chiseled features, and no shirt. My, my, my! I flip the page and he has a couple more pictures, this time half-naked holding what looks like a hose in front of his hose. Damn! Y'all show all that, hell show the rest! I scream to myself! Man, men in uniform do something to me. Something unexplainable. Shit unimaginable! I'm feeling tingling in my lady garden. Wish Dev was here to try something new. Like, let's sixty-nine and shit. Grant it I have the slightest idea how that feels, but at this present moment, I'm willing to try it! Fuck it. The girls on porn seem to enjoy the hell out of it. Where's my damn vibrator?! I get up and walk to my nightstand, find it, grab the toy cleaner, and sit on the side the bed. I turn it on. VRMM MM MMMMMM VRMM MM MMMMM. I turn it off and spray the cleaner on it and clean it. I guess some would call me a freak, and others just plain nasty, but I really don't recall cleaning it before I left for Vegas! Hell, he probably doesn't know who the hell I am anymore because of all the sex I've been having with Dev. The crazy part is, he doesn't satisfy me every time. Most of the time I may climax once a day, and fake all the rest. I wipe a little too hard and end up turning it on again. VRMM MM MMMMMM. Damn this thing don't know what it does to me! I feel like a wild tiger. Burning up on the inside ready to pounce. I look at my room door and realize I never locked it. I need to start getting in a habit of that. Someone is going to end up walking in on one of my escapades one day. I lay down my vibrator and walk over and lock it. I turn my music almost to maximum, 'cause for one, I don't want interruptions, and two, I may be a little noisy!

    I strip down in front of my body-length mirror to my panties and bra. Matching red set Victoria's secret type shit. Not really VS, but close enough. They serve their purpose! They turned Dev on so quickly I don't think they were on a whole five minutes. Hell, they turn my own ass on! I'm a hottie! CLASH! I hear a loud noise in the living room and become startled. Hell, more than startled. I think I jumped ten feet in the air. Like glass breaking or something. It freaks me out to know whatever it is, is louder than my music in my room. I go to my bedpost and grab my robe, go to my nightstand, and grab my 9 millimeter, check the bullets, and head to my room door. Turning the music down, all I hear now is silence. I quietly unlock my room door and crack it open enough to see down the hall. I probably should've left the music on, but now it's too late. I hold my gun like I see on movies. Straight up ready to pull the trigger. I'm ready to blast a motherfucker. I then enter the hallway not seeing anyone. I walk to the kitchen. That's where the noise came from I think. Inch by inch I inch along. Get to the kitchen and see no-one. I step on something sharp and gasp in pain. I look down and see broken glass. Shit! I tiptoe and inch around the bar, BING! I'm hit with something from behind and begin to fall seeing stars. What the hell?

I wake up with my head throbbing and tied to a chair. What in the hell? What happened?! I'm in my bra and panties and my robe is gone. I attempt to stand but realize my wrists are tied behind the wooden chair I'm sitting in. I try to lift my legs and learn they are also tied. "HELP! HELP ME! SOMEONE PLEASE!" I yell and begin crying. "HELP!" I hang my head down to my chest crying, trying to pull the rope on my wrists in the opposite direction. It hurts like hell, and I don't even think I've even done anything to the rope to loosen it. I reopen my eyes and twist my head to the back of me to attempt to see exactly what my hands are tied with. I can't. I attempt to rub my wrists together in hopes of loosening the knot or whatever has the hold of me and cant. All it does is burn like fire. I try to lift my feet, but they seem to be tied and attached to my wrists some way. "HELP! SOMEBODY, PLEASE COME HELP ME! IM TIED TO A CHAIR AND WAS JUST ROBBED! HELP," I yell from the top of my lungs. NOTHING. Still nothing. I honestly don't know if we were actually robbed, but you do what you have to do in situations like this. I begin to wonder how long I had been out. As I look around, I don't see anything missing or misplaced. I don't hear anything like anyone else is home. "JANAE! DEV! SOMEBODY! ANYBODY! PLEASE HELP ME!" I weep. "HELP! HEEEELP! HEEEEELP ME! IM TIED TO A CHAIR AND NEED HELP! HELLOOOOO! SOMEBODY, PLEASE HELP ME!" I yell and yell with not a single response. Janae or Devon should be coming home any minute now, right?

I wake up to the sound of keys jingling and being inserted in the door. "JANAE!"

"Boy, am I glad to see you!" I scream hoarsely. "Where have you been?!" I look at the kitchen window and notice that it's dark.

"Went on that date with Sam after work, remember?" I hear her say, walking over to the light switch. "Why you sitting in the dark like my mama waiting on me to get home?" she asks, flipping on the switch. She turns around to face me and gasp.

"What the hell, Jazmynn?" running over to me, attempting to untie me with no luck.

"I don't know how long I've been sitting here. I was playing my music in my room. Heard a noise…"

Crack, crack! "What the…" Janae says, walking on glass. She flips on the kitchen light over the sink. "What the hell happened?" she exclaims while grabbing a pair of scissors out of the drawer.

"I don't know! I heard a crashing sound and when I came out somebody must have hit me from behind. I woke up in this chair. I screamed and hollered but nobody heard me. I guess I cried myself to sleep," I say hoarsely. She has now cut one hand loose and is finishing up the other. I rub both wrists where the rope held me hostage. They are red and burned from rubbing against the rope. She cuts at the rope on my ankles, and I am finally free. I stand sort of weak, from sitting all those hours not being able to move. Janae grabs the first-aid kit from the storage closet in the hall and tells me to sit as she begins to move my hair around and starts dabbing something cold and wet in my head. It begins to sting and I wince at the pain. She then says, "Okay, that's fine for now. Hopefully, you don't need stitches." I turn and hug Nae Nae. She hugs back and lets me go taking a deep breath going to the phone.

"What are you doing?" I ask.

"Calling the police!" she exclaimed.

"Okay," I say. "I will look around to see if anything is missing. I kind of skimmed the room of what I could while I was tied up but, everything looked in place, I will check my room and yours. Hopefully, we can get in touch with Dev and have him check his, 'cause you know his door is always locked," I say walking toward Janae's room.

I heard someone at the door and immediately become scared. They wiggle the doorknob, stop, then do it again. We then hear a light tap. "Open up," the ruff voice says outside the door.

"Who is it?" I ask, running back to the kitchen getting a butcher knife out of the kitchen drawer. Janae tiptoes to the hall closet grabbing her forty-five off the top shelf.

"Dev," says the voice.

"Who?" I asked, beginning to shake with my eyes wide.

"Ah, hm, Dev," the voice answers louder and a little more clearly.

I drop the knife on the cabinet and I fly to the door. I open the door and run straight into his arms. Safety. I know I'm safe now.

"Uh, what's up with you?" he asked a little startled with a slight smirk on his face.

"My friend is searching the apartment now but nothing that I know of so far. She was assaulted. When I arrived she was tied to a chair in her undergarments. About thirty minutes? Are you kidding me?! THIS IS AN EMERGENCY, BITCH! What? Yeah, okay. All right. Um-Hm. Yeah, all right, whatever. Thanks."

Janae slams the phone down on the base. "People make me fucking sick!" she yells.

"Somebody broke in," I begin to tell Dev. "And hit me from behind. I woke up tied to a chair! I've been there for hours screaming for help," I begin to cry. My voice is so hoarse, he barely understands me.

"What?" he asks.

"Somebody broke in, Dev. They tied her to a chair. I called the police and they are on their way." Janae repeats in her own words for me.

"Why?" Dev asked, pushing me away by my shoulders.

"W-what? Why what?" I ask in total disbelief.

"Why did you call the police? Did they take anything?" he asks, seemingly more scared than concerned.

"So far no," I say. "I'm not done checking the house." I turn away from him to continue my search.

"Why wouldn't we call the cops?!" Janae asked. "Some motherfucker has broken into our home and assaulted Jazmynn! Who knows if they haven't stolen anything?" Nae Nae says, annoyed at Dev's question looking around the house checking for missing items.

"Well, I didn't say it right. What I meant was, is anything missing? 'Cause like, if not, they (the police) probably won't do much of anything. Did he talk, did you see him, or did you hear him say anything Jazmynn?" Dev asked.

"No, all I heard was the glass breaking on the floor, but, I still want to file a report. That was a horrible experience being tied to a chair for hours with no help. Maybe there are fingerprints on the glass they can take for evidence, I don't know. But I can't let this go. I no longer feel safe at home alone!" I say, heading to the restroom to clean my face.

A few minutes pass when Janae knocks on the bathroom door and tells me two officers are here to take my statement.

"Good evening, Mrs. Barkley, we understand you are a victim of a break in. Can you tell us exactly what happened?"

"I was in my room and listening to the radio when I heard the sound of glass breaking. I jumped up, grabbed my gun, and went to the kitchen where I heard the noise come from. Then I was hit behind my head with something and woke up tied to that chair," pointing to their left. "I screamed in hopes of someone passing by that would hear, but I guess no one did. I cried myself to sleep and woke up to my roommate Janae opening the door. She untied me and we called you," I say, pointing to them. One of them scribbled away in a notebook, and the other is sweeping the room with his eyes.

"Is anything missing?" one of them asked.

"No," I say, looking questioningly at Janae.

"No, my things haven't been touched," she answers.

"Ma'am," says the other cop, "you stated you had a gun, where is it? Did you at any time discharge your weapon at the suspect?"

"No, I didn't have the chance to. I was hit from behind. I wish I did though, I would have killed that bastard!"

"So where is the weapon, ma'am? We need to get the serial number and run it as a routine check…"

"Um… Well…" I get up and look around the kitchen floor. Where the chair was. Under the sofa. And all over the living room. No gun.

"Actually, Officers," I say with one hand on my hip and the other scratching my head. "It is missing."

"Your gun is missing?" asks the officer who has been scribbling away in his notebook.

"Yes, sir, I didn't notice it at first. Well, I kind of forgot all about it after everything happening. I thought I had done a pretty extensive search. I believe it's the only thing missing," I say.

"Okay, ma'am. Would you happen to have your paperwork for your gun with you so we can put an alert out that it has been stolen? If the perpetrator attempts to sell your weapon to a pawn shop if it's used in a crime, or sold to anyone else it will pop up in our system."

I immediately leave, go to my room in my nightstand, and grab my ownership papers. When I return, I ask, "Okay, I'm giving you the only paperwork I have for my weapon, that is stolen. When will I receive my paperwork back to show as proof of ownership if you do find my weapon?"

"Actually, ma'am, we only need information off the paperwork. We don't need to take it. If you're available tomorrow to bring a copy that will be even better, but we just want a few numbers and information off of it, you can keep it."

They got their information, bid me farewell, and was out the door. I took some sleeping meds and went to bed. Man! What a day!

Chapter 15

It's fashion week!

Top designers from all over the country will be presenting their new fashion lines having high-end fashion shows, presentations, and more at the Hilton on Riverside this week. Guest speaker Peter Williamson will be presenting his new skirts for shirts line Saturday at 7:00 p.m. For more information on tickets, times and dates of the events, please go to the fashion show website @neworleansfashionshow2012.com you don't want to miss it!

Oh, wow. Peter is in town? I say to myself closing the newspaper and placing it down on my desk. I look out at my office of empty seats. The free hours go so slow and it's almost as though I'm not really needed. I don't get many students in here. I guess all is well with their lives and they don't have anything they need to talk about. I walk over to the window and look outside at students walking to and from classes. I sigh. That was once me. I begin to think about the fact I think I want to see Peter. I have so many questions to ask him. Why did he take a swing at Dev? Was it some sort of jealousy thing? I'm glad to know he's better. I just hate the fact they got into it for no reason. I really wish he would answer his texts…

I'm so glad to be home. Today was a long day. Walking in, "Hey, Nae Nae. Where's Dev?" I ask, looking around at what seems to be an empty apartment.

She shrugs her shoulders, smacking her lips, continuing looking at her magazine. "Girl I don't know. I don't keep tabs on your man."

"He's not here though, is he?" I ask, a little suspicious.

"No," she answers, sounding completely uninterested turning the page.

"Okay, well check this out. Did you read the paper today?" I ask, plopping down on the couch beside her.

"No, why?" she asks, pulling her blanket back over her feet.

"Well, because this week is fashion week and guess who's in town?"

"Who?" she looks up from her magazine.

"Peter! He's going to be a guest speaker Saturday and will be introducing a new line he has. We should go!" I say looking at her facial expression.

"Uh, Jazmynn, I don't really think that's a good idea. Have you forgotten what happened the last time he and Dev were in the same room together?" She looks back, raising both eyebrows laying down her magazine on the coffee table.

"No, I haven't forgotten," I say, "I meant me and you go and don't tell Dev," I answer with a sneaky grin on my face.

"I still don't know," she says with one finger on her lip like she's in deep thought. "I mean, for one, how are you going to get away from Dev, and two, how you don't know he won't find out?" she asks.

"Well," I say, "maybe we can tell him we want to have a little girl's night. Keep a low profile at the fashion show, he shouldn't suspect anything or be able to find out anything? Right? I mean, I don't know. I really need to talk to Peter, though. I have so many unanswered questions, and I can't tell if Dev is lying or if it really went how he says it went. Plus that time someone broke into our house. I mean, Peter has the funds to have something like that done, right?"

"Even if we go, how are you certain you will see Peter, or more or less be able to talk to him? How do you know he will even talk to you? How do you know he's not pissed with you, or that he will be the one lying? Girl, this shit can take a turn for the worst real fast. You better make sure this is exactly what you want to do. Personally, I think you should give it up and let it go. You sent flowers when he was in the hospital. You've done your good deed, just let it all be!" she says, throwing one hand toward her lap. "And what would make you think Peter was the one broke into the house? That just doesn't make sense. Hell, he knows where you are from, not where you live, Jazmynn," she says, rolling her eyes like she's never seen someone so stupid.

"I know what you're saying, but I need to know! Maybe it's stupid, I don't care. Are you down or not?" I ask while I roll my eyes back, annoyed.

"Okay," she answers, throwing both hands in the air. "Yeah, I'll go, but nothing good will come from it. Just watch."

She's upset. I know. But she'll get over it. I'm just glad she's going to come with me, and I don't have to make up a reason to lie to Dev even worse than the reason I have to now.

We are watching Maury when Dev comes through the door. He looks a little strange. Angry?

"You okay?" I ask.

"Yeah, I'm fine," he huffs. But something is wrong. Something is definitely wrong. He walks down the hall to the bathroom, so I get up to go meet him. "Are you sure you're okay?" I ask. "I said I was, didn't I?" he answers sarcastically. "Okay… You seem like something is bothering you. I will let you be. Before I forget, Janae and I are having a girls night Saturday night." And I walk away. He mumbles something I couldn't hear, but who cares. I don't know what has his panties in a wad, but the hell with him. He has an attitude and I don't have time for it.

Saturday

We arrive at the Hilton dressed to impress almost as though we are models ourselves. Nae Nae got us a limousine 'cause she said it would be tacky to show up in a regular car being that so many famous people would be here. The limo driver pulls up to the red carpet and photographers are swarming each side impatiently waiting to see who exits the limo. I take a deep breath. I can do this. I smile at Nae Nae who is dressed in a black bodysuit with gold body jewelry and sparkling gold six-inch heels. She is wearing the hell out of that suit. She has the breasts for the low-cut, three-inch slit in the front, and the ass that's the right size for the suit. Not too big and not too small. I mean it's just right! She has some long gold chandelier earrings and a bracelet to match. Her hair is natural as it always is but seems fuller with those beautiful curls. I, on the other hand, decided to wear semi baggy denim jeans that are folded at my ankles with a white half shirt and brown cargo-type half-sleeve jacket with khaki boot heels. I have a long owl necklace that hangs a little below my breasts with a leopard print, with earrings and a bracelet to match. It's sort of an urban style, but it's me!

The limo driver comes to the side door of the carpet and stands with his back to us. People are lining up behind us to be dropped off, and I began to wonder, *What the hell?*

"Why hasn't he opened the door?" I ask Janae.

"Hell, I don't know! I mean, I know we don't open it ourselves, right?" she asks, looking at me, puzzled.

"Maybe we should put a crack in the window and tell him we are ready to walk out?" I say.

The privacy window rolls down. There's a man in the driver seat, but all we can see is the back of his head.

"Are you ready to exit yet, ladies?" he asked.

"Oh, wow!" Janae exclaims. "I so didn't know you were up there! There are two of you?" she asks.

"Yes, ma'am," he answers. "I drive and he ushers and does the security ma'am."

"So he stays with us the whole night?" I asked, puzzled.

"Yes, ma'am, we both sort of do. I stay with the car and he stays with you guys. It is your choice if you would rather no security ma'am…" he says.

I turn to Janae. "Should we? This will be fun!" I say excitedly.

"Sure. Okay," Janae says.

He closes the window and our security for the night turns to open our door. He is dressed in a lavish suit. He's not too handsome but seems kind enough.

Screams on top of screams. The photographer and paparazzi go wild. You would think we were famous or something! Janae steps out first and models a little letting the cameras get every angle of her bodacious body. Then I step out. The camera lights are so bright, but it doesn't bother me because, at this moment, I feel so authoritative. Our security for the night closes our door and stands arms folded and head down behind us. I whisper in Janae's ear we should start walking. As we do reporters are screaming questions at us like who we're wearing. Who are we? Were we secret models? We just smiled, waved, and kept walking. Once inside the mood was a lot quieter. A hostess stood by the entrance with a tray and glasses of champagne. We each grabbed one and walked toward the entrance that the fashion show would be held. It got a lot louder once we actually entered from music playing over a speaker. There were many people sitting at tables, around the runway, and what looked to be VIP because they had couches.

We find a spot right next to the runway and almost run that way. Once seated, we realize there were only two seats, and our security was standing behind us.

Janae turns to him and asks if he would like us to move to a place that had three seats, but he declined reminding her he was working and it was a part of his job. He promised he would stay out of the way of people behind us so they could enjoy the show without him interrupting.

The runway was lit up the brightest of lights I have ever seen. It also changed colors with the beat of the music. We are going to have a blast! I can feel it!

Janae starts to look around and leans over and asks, "Do the waiters pass so people can buy drinks? This little glass of water is gone already!" I laugh and begin to look around to see if I could see anyone like the girl at the front door. Nothing. I feel a tap on my shoulder and it's the security guy.

"Huh?" I say.

"Can I help you find someone?" he asks in a deep voice. Like deep, deep. Like Michael Clark Duncan deep.

I smile at him. That's kind of sexy. "No, well yeah, kind of. We're looking for a waiter."

"What will you have?" he asks.

"Uh, well, I'll have a Tom Collins and she'll have crown with a splash of Coke," I say

He nods and walks away. Returning within minutes with our drinks, he hands each to us and we thank him.

The lights go off and it's almost completely dark and a spotlight shines toward where the models will be coming out. I'm so excited! A lady walks out microphone in hand, wearing a long bulky uneven-ed dress and begins to speak.

"Good evening, ladies and gentleman! Welcome to the New Orleans 2012 Fashion Extravaganza! Tonight you will see the fashions of Michael Kors, Louis Vuitton, Sean Paul, and more just to name a few. Our guest speaker whom will grace us with his presence a little later will be also introducing a new line of his own 'Skirts for Shirts.' Everyone, please help me welcome the first line to be presented by Sean Paul and his strawberry sweetcakes!"

The crowd applauds in unison as women begin to walk out and strut their stuff. I see them more as entertainers than models because some of them aren't physically cute. That's wrong to say, but a woman's physical appearance really does matter in fashion. The next designs come out. And then the next until I've lost count. Fireworks begin to explode and let us know we've made it to the finale.

"Ladies and gentlemen, let's put our hands together and welcome our guest speaker Mr. Peter Williamson on the stage."

Applause.

He walks out on stage dressed in a white suit with purple gator shoes, a silk purple shirt, and a purple hat. Like Barney purple. It's ugly. Real ugly.

"Good evening everyone. My name is Peter Williamson and tonight I will be presenting to you my new skirts for shirts fashion line. You guys are in for a treat. See, I'm not your average Joe!" Laughter from the crowd. "I know what men want to see a woman in, and I know what women need to complement their body shapes."

He walks further down the stage closer to where we are sitting. The Barney purple isn't so bad at all. It suits him and compliments his body shape! He is more handsome than the last time I saw him!

He scans his eyes through the crowd, almost as though he's attempting to make eye contact with every person in the building.

"I will be having an after-party at this exact location. Please give me your feedback and let me know what you think and how you like the designs I have…"

He looks right at me. Shocked at first, but then almost as though he's happy to see me. You can almost hear crickets. He's just staring and smiling at me. He then says, "Ladies and gentlemen, look at this beautiful woman right here. You've given me inspiration! Ma'am, if you would, would you allow me to design something in the back for you? Just to show the audience how well I do my job. How I'm fast and efficient, and how my line compliments every woman's body shape?"

I know he didn't! All eyes are on me. Literally. The spotlight shines on me and my face is plastered on TVs all over the room. I can't believe this. I'm so embarrassed. People are applauding and shouting Go! Go! Go! Go! Janae nudges me and leans over, "You want me to go for you?" she asks jokingly. "Go on, girl! Show 'em what you got!" and she pulls my arm to aid me in standing.

"Sure," I answer, making the crowd grow wild.

Peter walked toward one side of the runway and extended his hand out showing me there were steps leading up to the stage. The security walked with me that way and probably would've walked on stage too, but I turned back and said, "I'm okay." So he held my left hand up the stairs and Peter grabbed the other. The whole time the spotlight is following my every step. Peter ushers me to the center of the stage and twirls me like a ballerina.

"Honestly, people, I don't really know if I can do any better than what's already done. This woman is already the bomb.com! But"—releasing my hand out of the air and placing his in his pocket still holding the microphone in his other hand—"I will let you guys have your own opinion. Please welcome my models modeling skirts for shirts to the stage! Enjoy the show, everyone!"

He waves at the crowd and we exit the stage grabbing me by my waist with his left hand and turning the microphone off with the right. Once backstage, I realize this is a whole other show in itself. There are topless women running all around, a gay guy screaming because he said a model must've eaten a snickers before fitting, and makeup artists doing makeup next to big mirrors with gigantic lightbulbs.

He pulls me into his room. Obviously, because it says Peter Williamson. It's so much quieter in here. There's four full-length mirrors almost in a square, and I run to it first. Seems so cool. I can see the front of me and the back of me at the same time if I turn in the correct angle!

"You like that?" asks Peter, pouring a shot of scotch in a glass. He then walks over to an ice bucket, uses some tongs to put some ice in his glass, and turns back to me. "Drink?" he asks, sipping his scotch.

"Yes and yes please," I say, moving away from the mirror. I realized I must have looked conceited. Lord knows I'm the complete opposite. I walk over and sit on the couch waiting for my drink. I need to go ahead and have this conversation. Hell that's what I'm here for, right?

"Ahm." I clear my throat. "How have you been?" I ask as he hands me a glass of zinfandel and he sits on the right side of me.

"I've been well," he says. I guess he's not giving up any kind of information without me outright asking for it. So here it goes.

"I sent you some flowers while you were in the hospital. Did you get them?" I asked, taking a sip of wine.

"Yes, I certainly did," he answers. "Would've been a whole lot easier to send a thank you card if there was an address to send it to…" he says, smiling.

"I'm sorry. That part was Janae. She told the lady to just put my message and nothing more." I take another sip. This is some really good wine. The grape flavor is so crisp. "So anyway," I begin, "I've tried to text you a few times, and I noticed in the paper you would be here tonight and I wanted to come to see you and ask you a few questions if you don't mind." I look down at my shoes. I bet this is not what he was expecting. Moving closer to me lifting my chin to face him, "I'm at your disposal." In the sexiest way possible. Dev who? I wonder. I can totally devour this dude at this moment. But that's not why I'm here. So time to get down to business. I pull back from his gentle hold and begin.

"So what exactly happened between you and Devon the night you were, uh, in the altercation?" I ask.

"Well, after I left from dancing with you I had to go drain the pipe." The pipe. Hmmm. I would like to see that pipe. I smile.

"And while I was in the restroom handling my business, your friend Devon walked in. I introduced myself as Peter, the owner, and told him I knew you and Janae. I told him if there was anything else I could do to accommodate you guys stay to let me know. He sort of mean mugged me and went into a stall. I moved to the full-length mirror to adjust my clothes while he handled his business. When he came out, I told him I meant no disrespect. He said none taken and walked out so I thought we were cool. I was in the restroom for a few more minutes and he walked back in. Before I walked out I turned to him, went to shake his hand, and told him he was a lucky guy to have as gorgeous of a woman as you, and he went ballistic. He asked me what the fuck I meant by that. Was I trying to say he didn't deserve you? Was I trying to say he didn't have any money? I told him no, I was only complimenting him, but he seemed to already be on the defensive end when he walked into the restroom. I really should have kept my mouth closed, but I honestly meant no harm. He then tackled me into the restroom door, we wrestled a little, the whole while I'm telling him he's tripping. Before I knew it he slammed my head against the mirror and kicked the vanity off the wall, having water shoot all over then ran out of the restroom. I stood up and began to wet a napkin to wipe my face when he came in again. I figured he wasn't done and wanted to fight some more and swung at him first. He then started tripping asking me what the hell was I doing, but I didn't stop so we fought again. I heard the door to the restroom open and all I remember is waking up in the hospital."

I'm sitting there with my mouth on the floor. He's saying Dev was defensive, but Dev said the complete opposite? Dev said Peter swung at him first, and he was just defending himself. That, which was why Peter dropped the charges because he knew he was wrong!

"Well, Dev said you swung first, and that, that was the reason you dropped the charges. Because you knew you were out of line," I say, puzzled.

"Jazmynn, there was no need for me to cause conflict with Devon. I don't even know the guy and don't really care to. I introduced myself because I was a little curious of who could capture such a wonderful woman because honestly I really like you and would love to get to know you better but you have already laid your platform and told me you are in a relationship. I respect that. The women I've dated never gave me the respect you do for Devon and I guess that's what draws me to you. Truthfully, I don't think you have yourself about nothing but a jealous piece of a shit bipolar boyfriend with anger issues, but hey, that's your choice," he says, shrugging his shoulders.

"I don't know what to say! I mean, so Dev has been lying to me all this time?" I say and kill the rest of my glass of wine and shake my head in disappointment. He gets up, straightening his clothes. "I have no reason to lie to you." He grabs my glass out of my hand and goes to refill it.

But I'm still puzzled! I turn toward him. "Then, why did you drop the charges?! I'm lost!" I exclaimed, throwing my hands up. "Honestly," he says taking a deep breath while walking back over to me. "Because I couldn't remember all the details. The police said your boyfriend's story and my story didn't add up." He hands me my refilled glass. "Well, it added up to a certain extent. See, I sort of remembered the restroom door opening, and what looked as though him walking out, but then I began to see two of him and it's like he was having a disagreement with himself," he says, pacing the floor almost as if he was re-living the events. "I thought I was tripping and was having double vision from the last big hit I received, but I swore I heard voices like, "What are you doing here?" and some other gibberish. It was like he was fighting himself!" he says, turning to me with a strange expression on his face. "I know it may sound ridiculous or crazy, but it's what I think I heard and saw! I had been hit hard!" he says, turning away from me once more. "The police were adamant about the fact that no one but your boyfriend entered or exited the restroom at that time. But knowing what I thought I remembered, how could I press charges on him?" he says, flipping his left hand up to the ceiling. "I wasn't in my correct state of mind. I mean, it could have easily been someone else to knock me out after the fact. You know? An angry customer or anybody. Then the way the police were talking was like your boyfriend didn't know anything that had happened." He then places his left hand in his left pocket. "They said he was highly intoxicated, seemed high on drugs, and couldn't even tell them how he got where he was when he was found. Either way, I felt no need to press charges because the whole altercation would've been avoided if I would've just kept my mouth shut," he says rubbing the rim of his glass after taking a sip.

Taking a deep breath as though a weight has been lifted off of his chest he turns to me. "Anyway, beautiful, it's time to change the subject. We can finish this conversation at a later time if you don't mind, but I have some designing to do. Have you ever modeled?" he asked with a twinkle in his eye and a handsome smile on his face.

"No." I giggle like a little school girl. "But I mean, it can't be all that hard," I say while straightening my posture.

"Okay, miss, I got this," he says. "I need you down to your panties and bra. And before you think I'm just trying to get a good look at your sexy ass body, I am, but I also need you with no clothes on to design an outfit," he says flirtatiously and businesslike all at once. I blush. Thank goodness I have matching under clothes and wasn't lazy when I got dressed tonight. 'Cause, lawd, I would be so embarrassed! "Okay," I say shyly, "but do you have a robe?"

"In the bathroom," he answered. "I will be right back, I need to go get one of my pre-designed shirts," and out the door, he went.

I go in the bathroom where there are towels stacked on the vanity but can't find the robe. I realize I need to pee, so I close the door and go to the toilet. After looking back at the door, I realize the robe is hanging there. Great! I say. I sure the hell didn't want to be just sitting on the couch in my bra and panties waiting for him to return. I finish my business, undress, put on the robe, and return to the living room area. I pour myself another glass of wine and wonder exactly how long I had been in here. Janae is watching the whole runway by herself! I hope she's not upset with me. I go back to the bathroom to grab my clothes and put them on the couch, because soon as I walk out and model whatever he puts on me, I'm coming to get back dressed and going back to meet her.

After doing that task, I realize I'm getting a little sleepy. I need a pick-me-upper. I go to the mini fridge and see several Red Bull energy drinks, so I grab one and pop it open. Gulping it down, Peter returns back to the room and drops his jaw.

"So this is what you do? You go into people's rooms and raid their mini bars and drink their drinks without invitation?" he asks jokingly.

"I am so sorry," I say. "I can pay for it, I just started yawning and couldn't stop and didn't want to keep drinking wine without something to help keep me up, because otherwise, I will pass out wherever I sit!" I say apologetically. I feel so embarrassed. I wasn't thinking! Like really? Who does that? I frown scorning myself.

"Girl, its fine!" he laughs. "Give me one while you're over there," he says and I do.

When I hand him the Red Bull, he grabbed my hand instead of the can and pulled me to him. He hugged me so gently, so manly, so innocently. I couldn't push away. I like it. He smelled of Perry Ellis 360. Another personal favorite I have. I inhaled deeply into his chest. Mesmerizing. MMMMMM... I say out loud. Not meaning to, I really tried to keep that to myself.

He steps back. "Are you okay? Was that out of place? I apologize, Jazmynn. I sincerely do. I know you have a boyfriend and all, but I sort of needed a hug. No excuse for my action, I know. If you want to leave, I understand," He says actually looking sincere. Leave? Hell nah! Let me sniff you some more! "No, I'm fine. I guess I kind of needed a hug too," I say.

"Okay, let's get started," he says while rubbing his hands together and taking a step back. He turns around to the couch where he had put some fabric when he first walked in and holds up a piece of red and black fabric that looked like a skirt. I guess Skirts for shirts was literally what it is!

"Step into this," he says, handing it to me.

I take it and pull it up under the robe, fighting to stay covered, which it falls back to the floor. "What size is it?" I ask almost insulted.

"Take off your robe," he says, laughing. "I have to design it, remember? I'm going to make it your size." Before I do, I step out of the skirt, hand it to him, and grab my half glass of wine. So what if, he was calling me skinny? I have a buzz, I don't give a damn!

I kill the rest of my wine then drop my robe. His eyes start to race my body like race cars. Up and down and left to right. He then blushes!

"I, uh, I, well…" he stutters.

"What's wrong? Cats got your tongue?" I asked, licking my bottom lip really slowly.

"Oh no! No, I'm fine." He says still staring me up and down. I begin to see a bulge in his pants. Haha. He's excited. I giggle a little bit and he comes back to earth and steps up to me. Kiss me! I know you want to. Hell, I know I want you to. But he doesn't. He immediately puts on his business face and gets to work. At least until he touched my left breast. "Oh, uh, sorry," he mumbled. Continuing his work he brushed across each breast and my ass several times saying, "Sorry or excuse me." Until I was completely covered. He turned the skirt into a sort of one-shouldered dress that had scissor slits in the front above my breasts and slits right above my ass. He makes the slits toward the lower part of the dress, then tied them some kind of way together. It actually was pretty cute. As he was finishing up I asked him, "How long have I been in here?"

"About an hour. You haven't missed much I promise. I got my models to model some of last year's designs, and they don't even know it. Hold on…" He walked to the door and told the guy standing outside something and came back to me to fix little odd and end pieces he didn't like. He walks over to the fridge and pours me a half glass of wine while saying, "You will walk out in two minutes… Aw, shit! Shoes!" he yells running up to me with my glass and then out of the room. Within seconds, he returned with some black heels that tie up that looked like they were ten inches high!

"Oh, hell no! There ain't no way I will be able to walk in those," I say.

"Just sit," he answered. "I will put them on you and you can try and see." I sit, sipping on my wine. It doesn't matter if he puts them on or if I put them on, they are still going to be too tall!

He finishes the shoes and helps me stand. I take a step to walk, and then another, and another. They aren't bad at all!

"I designed these too." He smiled with appreciation and I laugh. He is really talented.

I walk over to the full-length mirrors and look at myself. The shit is hot! I look great. I turn one way then the other. Everything looks so perfect. There's a tap at the door and it's a female with something in her ear I guess is like a walkie-talkie. She tells Peter its time. He walks up to me, turns me around, and teases certain areas of my hair giving it volume. Then it happened. Completely unexpected. He kisses me. Not with a lot of tongue like Dev does all forcefully, but gently. Like he's massaging my tongue. His lips are so soft, in the middle of the kiss, I bite his bottom lip gently. "MMM..." he says.

"Uhm, uhm..." he says pulling away from me taking a couple steps back. "Uhm, uhm, girl, whooo! That right there?!" He points at me. "Uh-uh. No can do. No can do!" he says, shaking his finger at me, but sounding like he's trying to convince himself.

Now grant it, I know this is wrong, but this moment feels so right. I'm so attracted to him, and I can tell the feelings are mutual. I walk enclosing the space between us and kiss him on the lips. Once. Then once more. He begins to kiss back, and I bite his lip again moaning. With a smile on my face, I turn away from him walking out of the door.

As I walked out the girl who came to the door earlier grabbed my right hand and pulled me to an entrance telling me to walk to out on the beat. I begin to walk out and feel someone grab my left arm, and I fall back. I'm caught by Peter! He kisses me a little harder this time, and it means something. What? Phew. I know my face is flustered when he stands me back upright and nudges me to go out on stage.

I step out on the beat, walk to the beat, and pause here and there for photos. Janae is on her feet clapping and yelling, "That's my best friend yall!' The crowd is going crazy. They must love it. A couple photographers hand signaled for me to turn different angles and I do. I smile for a couple photos and do a few serious face poses. I really like this modeling shit. I feel special. All eyes are on me and I'm the center of attention! The crowd begins to scream even louder and I turn to see Peter coming onto the stage. No wonder they're going so crazy! Haha! He has changed into dark stone-wash blue jean shorts with a navy blue button-down T-shirt and some blue Jordan's to match. I stand there smiling at him and it almost seems as though no one else is in the room but us. Until someone grabs my ankle pulling me. I glance down, and at first, my heart dropped. I opened my mouth in awe. I thought it was Devon! I begin to fall toward the crowd and Peter sees and comes sweeping me off my feet spinning me around before finally putting me back down in the center of the stage. The crowd goes even crazier. I notice my security and a couple other guys in suits surrounded a man telling him to leave. They grabbed him by both arms while he was kicking and yelling something. My security punches him in the face knocking him out and the guys all grab a part of him and carry him out. Poor guy. I doubt he meant any harm, but he liked to have given me a heart attack at first glance. As soon as this is over, Janae and I need to leave. That was a little too close for comfort. If Dev found out I was here at Peter's event, who knows what he would do? Hell if he found out about the kisses, one of us would probably die. Either Peter or me...

"Ladies and gentlemen, I am Peter Williamson once again and we are back with the finished product. Now I must say, this was a workout," he says, twirling me to show all his work. "This woman's body is a piece of art. I mean, man. This was the best body to ever do a quick piece of fashion clothing on." He winks at the crowd and majority of the guys laugh and throw the thumbs-up sign. "I wanted to put a little something here." He points at my ass, causing the guys in the audience to go wild and begin whistling. "But why in the hell would I want to cover that up?" Crowd bursts into laughter again. "Anyway"—steadily giggling—"I hope you all enjoyed this piece and the whole fashion show. This will conclude the New Orleans Fashion Show of 2012. Don't forget the after-party is held here as well and all are invited! Well, except the moron who tried to pull my model off the stage!" He chuckles. "Good night to all!" he says, waving to the crowd.

Loud music comes on and all the models walk back out to the beat doing their last walk. I put my hand on Peter's right shoulder and push down a little to make him bend to me giving me his ear. "Hey, can Janae come on stage and come to the back while I change?" I ask.

"Sure," he says, nodding toward a security guy and pointing at Janae, then motioning for her to come on the stage. The security guy walks to her and points to us. I wave my hand, mouthing, "Come up here." And she does. Our security follows but Peter's security stops him. They say a couple words to each other and Peter's security waves his hand in the air to catch Peter's eye. Peter turns to me and asks, "Is he with ya'll too?!" I nod yes. Then he says sarcastically, "He's not going to want to fight me in the restroom, is he?"

"Haha," I say. "No, he's our security silly!"

Peter turns back, chuckling and nods approval to allow our security up.

Backstage, Janae is in heaven. She moves from one makeup artist to the next asking all sorts of questions and getting either phone numbers or email addresses. I tap her shoulder, "Sorry to interrupt," I say to the other girl, "Are you ready to go to the room so I can change back into my clothes?" I ask Janae.

"Oh sorry! Yeah, girl! Girl, I'm in makeup artist heaven right now! My bad!" laughing aloud. I motion for her to follow me. I don't know where Peter went, but I do know where the room is, so I head that way. I turn the knob, but just as I thought it's locked. Our security asks did I forget my key. "No, It's not exactly my room." I giggle. He looks confused but steps back and stands behind us with his arms crossed.

"Is this Peter's room? 'Cause, girl, if he done put you up in your own room that fast..." Janae asked.

"Yeah," I said, cutting her off. "But I don't know where he went!" I continue. "I need to get my clothes and change. I'm keeping this fit though! Hell, it was made personally for my body type," I said, smiling from ear to ear a mischievous smile.

"Uh-huh," Janae says. "I know that look, don't forget you got a man at home!" she whispers the last part and bursts into laughter.

Yeah right, my new man is walking straight up to me!

Peter apologized for the wait and immediately opened the door.

"Make yourselves comfortable. There are a couple of clothing carts in the other room if you ladies would like to raid them. Feel free to change or take some to go. There are to-go bags already made on the table over there"—pointing behind us—"with different makeup and jewelry. Everything is for ya'll, so if your security needs help to bring anything down, let me know. I have to step out for a few minutes. Are you guys staying for the after party?"

"Yes."

"No," I said no; Janae said yes. He turns his head to the side, "Well, whatever you guys decide." He smiles and heads to the door. He places his hand on the knob then turns around and walks up to me. He smiles and leans over and lightly kisses me on the lips and rubs his left thumb on my left cheek. Oooohhh, weeee! Can you say weak in the knees?

"Oooooooooooooohhhh," Janae says, cupping her mouth, giggling. He glances at her and does a sexy side smile, then turns and walks to the door and leaves.

Janae ends up going home alone with our new wardrobe. We figure our stories where if Dev asks anything we're on the same page. The story is, I got drunk and got a room because I couldn't make it home, and Janae is supposed to pick me up in the morning. I know our story won't really work because Dev knows Janae ain't leaving me anywhere, but fuck it. Luckily when she got home, he was nowhere to be found. I ended up spending the night with Peter at the hotel. We laughed, kissed, and talked until the sun came up and I told him I needed to go. It was amazing! It was wrong but felt so right and the most awesome thing about the night was that Peter wanted no more than time spent. He never even tried to make a move although I would've probably let him go all the way!

We exchanged the correct phone numbers, and I got a taxi home.

Chapter 16

All I can do is think about Saturday night! My days in my office just breeze by. I haven't had many students to come in lately. Which is a good and bad thing. All in all, they are all bright students with level heads on their shoulders. I have no favorites, but there is one I do admire. She reminds me so much of myself. She stays in her books, and when she walks to and from classes, there is a guy that tries to get her attention but she like me, is always on her phone. I hope he doesn't wear her down like John did me. It will probably be a huge mistake as the one I made. There she goes again passing through. Not long from now will be graduation. She's probably so excited. Walking the opposite of her is a physique I've seen before. Is it? Nah, can't be. I wince to look closer and it definitely is. Peter! Oh my God! Oh my God! What will I do? I grab my pocket mirror to check my lipstick and see what condition my face is in. Today I wore some maroon skinnies, with brown knee-high boots. A maroon, brown, and beige pastel quarter-length button-down shirt with a beige cardigan. I take off the cardigan. It matches but takes away from how the shirt flows and hangs just right above my ass. I have my hair in two Indian braids and was getting ready to take them out so my hair could be wavy, but there was a knock at the door. I reach into my bag and find my Lucky You perfume and spritz my neck and wrist then say come in.

In walks ol' handsome Peter. Wow. Just as refreshing as the last time I saw him.

"Well, hi there, sir, to what do I owe this pleasure?" I smile, batting my eyes flirtatiously.

"My God, Jazmynn," walking up to me giving me a hug. "Girl, you get more beautiful every time I see you!" Then he kisses me on the cheek and steps back. "Well, I was wondering what you were doing for lunch?" he smiles.

"Not much, I brought a ham sandwich and some chips…" but before I could finish he responds, "Oh, ah-ah! No! Let's go! Lunch now, with me please?" He extends his right hand I take it, shrug my shoulders and say, "Why not?"

I grab my purse and follow him out of the door.

Honestly, I expected him to want to go to some five-star restaurant that served fancy food with wine and all the expensive shit, but soon as we got outside, he asked, "Mind taking a stroll? I know this place up the road, it's roughly a mile or so though. Named "Liuzza's by the track" with the best barbecue shrimp po'boys in New Orleans!" He must like to walk wherever he goes.

I check my watch I have roughly two hours for sure that are free, "Yeah, sure. It's a pretty day," I answered looking up at the sky. I know exactly where he's talking about and love the place. I get lunch there so often, they know my name when I walk through the door!

"It's actually one of my favorite places," I say. "I usually get the hot grilled chicken sub."

"Oh yeah?" he asks with the sexiest grin. It's a little warm today and amazingly this guy doesn't sweat. He glistens! Whooooo!

"So how have things been?" he asks casually.

"Everything has been good. How about yourself?" I ask, wondering how his wonderful life has been.

"Oh, everything is going swell! Business is booming, my new fashion line sales are through the roof, and I'm thankful. No reason to complain about anything my way," he says as we are walking through the entrance of the restaurant. The hostess walks up greeting me as usual. "Good afternoon, Ms. Barkley!"

"Hi there, Clara! How are you today?" I ask. She sighs, taking in a breath responding "Busy, busy, busy! Haha! Follow me, would you guys like a table or booth?" she asks. "A table is fine," I answer.

Once we are seated, we order our food and drinks. While waiting for our food to be delivered I ask, "So, Peter. You are a very successful man, established, and handsome. Why aren't you married with children in a big house with a picket fence?" I know I'm probably being a little too forward and its none of my business, but I really want to know! Like, is something wrong with him? Is he controlling? Maybe he can't be faithful? It has to be something.

"Well, Jazmynn. I haven't quite met the woman of my dreams yet, and without her, I can't have the children with the big house and picket fence." *Why?!* I scream inwardly.

"And why not?" I ask. Again none of my business. I wonder if my prying into his personal business is beginning to annoy him.

"Well, I really don't know. But when that woman does come into my life, it will make me the happiest man alive, and I will strive to be the best man a man can be to her because she will, of course, deserve that and more. So how's your relationship going? Wedding bells soon?" he snickers.

"Uh, no. No time soon," I say while rolling my eyes. Now he's prying in my life, and that doesn't feel so good.

"And why is that?" he asks, taking a sip of his drink.

"I don't know. I mean, we haven't been dating really, really long, but honestly, I hadn't thought about a future with Dev. Hell, we haven't even talked about it."

"Now see if I were dating you, our relationship would be clear as glass. You would know where our relationship stands. Girl, why don't you just go ahead and dump him so we can get us started?" He starts laughing. I go to respond, but he holds his hand up to stop me, "I'm kidding, girl. I respect you and your relationship. I don't want to, nor would I consciously do anything that would ruin it or jeopardize it because I wouldn't want it done to me. Your dude is a lucky one," he says, pointing his pinky at me. "I do know that. I just would like your friendship if that's okay with you?" he says.

"That's fine with me. Just know friend, you're paying for lunch today!" I start chuckling.

"Sounds fair," he says. "But you have the next one!" He laughs.

As we make it back to the school I check my watch and notice I have ten minutes until classes will begin. "Well, thank you for lunch. It was awesome. We should do it again some other time." I turn, facing him.

"It was my pleasure," he says, hugging me. "See you later!" he says, stepping back waiving while turning to walk away.

"Bye!" I wave back.

It's my turn to cook tonight. I look into the freezer to piece together a menu. Sausage, chicken, shrimp… Hell, I think I'm going to make a gumbo! I start making a roux and Dev comes up behind me kissing my neck, grabbing my ass, and hugging on me. I already know what time it is. We rarely talk anymore. All he wants is sex. At the beginning, I couldn't get enough of it myself, but now it's starting to seem more like a chore than it being fun. It's been a whole five months and every day it's the same thing. He comes home, sex. He eats, sex. He showers, sex. He wakes up, sex. SEX, SEX, SEX! It's the only thing that's constant in our relationship because each sexual event he does something different. I start thinking about the talk I had with Peter about marriage and realize, I don't want to spend the rest of my life doing nothing but having sex. I mean, we don't go anywhere anymore like we used to. We used to go out almost every weekend! He was like our bodyguard, but still. Now it's like we're a couple so we can't do those things anymore! Don't get me wrong, Janae and I still do stuff and go out here and there on the weekends, but he never wants to come with us. Then he gets pissed off that I'm leaving him. When I do decide to stay home, he goes to some bar. I don't know what he wants! Before I really knew him, not that I really know him now, he used to be so spontaneous. He would just up and tell us lets go take a trip or tell us he has tickets somewhere to get dressed and we end up going see plays like Porgy and Bess. Now nothing. I mean nothing. There's no romance, no dates, no gifts…

Finally. He walked away. Ugh! He's starting to get under my skin. I hate that. I find myself wondering if I love him. Before we were in a relationship, I just knew I was, but now I'm not too sure.

Janae comes into the kitchen and sits at the table. I feel her staring at me. What does she want? Haha!

"Yes?" I say, adding chicken broth to the pot stirring the bottom well to be sure nothing is sticking.

"Just looking," she says with her hands on her chin cocking her head to her side.

"Looking at?" I say, looking back at her with the spoon in my right hand.

"You. Is everything okay with you? You don't seem yourself lately…" she says, putting her hands down with a serious face.

"I'm fine. What do you mean?" I say. What is she talking about? Nothing has changed between me and her. Just the shit between me and Dev.

"You're not fine. You're the complete opposite. For whatever reason, you're not happy when you are home and it's written all over your face. Explain." She pretty much demands. "And before you say nothing and you're fine again, try with some other motherfucker. 'Cause I know you. I might just know you more than you know yourself. You look like you are hiding something. Bitch, are you pregnant?!" she says with her eyes as big as golf balls. She cups her mouth with both hands then drops them leaving her mouth ajar. There goes her little lightbulb in her head. She thinks she knows it all sometimes, but the poor thing is far off! I am most definitely not pregnant!

I glance toward Dev's room and look back at her. She catches the eye contact and scrunches up her face. "Do I need to set that motherfucker straight, 'cause I sholl will fuckin…" I hold my hand up for her to stop. "No, Nae Nae. Everything's fine, and I'm NOT pregnant," I say, trying to cut the conversation short and shut her up. But it's too late. She's already on her feet pointing her finger. Oh, Lord, here we go…

"What the fuck he did? Tell me! That's bullshit! I told you that motherfucker better not hurt you or I would…" She's screaming now. Oh shit, oh shit.

"JANAE!" I say over her throwing the spoon I'm cooking with on the stove. "Stop! Everything is fine!" At the same time, Dev comes out of his room, and oh shit. Oh shit, oh shit!

"YOU!" she yells, pointing at him glaring like she will lunge at him at any moment.

"What?" he asks, completely lost. Poor thing doesn't know what's about to hit him. Once she gets started, there's no stopping. NONE.

"The fuck you did her? You no good piece of shit? I knew she shouldn't have started dating you 'cause you wasn't gonna be worth a damn…"

"The fuck are you talking about, Janae?" he asks, immediately pissed. Like day and night. Red-faced, breathing like a bull, and ready to strike like a snake.

"I'm talking about Jazmynn…" she starts but I butt in. "Okay, Janae, you are blowing all of this out of proportion. I told you everything is fine."

"BULL FUCKING SHIT! That's bullshit!" she yells, throwing her right hand in the air.

"Bitch, who the fuck do you think you are talking to me like that?" Dev says, pointing at Nae Nae and starting to walk closer. "The fuck is your problem? Bitch…" He takes a deep breath and stops walking. "Fuck this shit." He turns toward the door and grabs his keys off of the key ring by the door. "Jazmynn, get your friends in line. I ain't 'bout dealing with no bullshit from no other bitch I ain't fucking and that ain't got shit to do with us." As he is grabbing the handle of the door, Nae Nae says, "You got one more bitch to call me before I fly over there and fuck you up!" She grabs a glass that was left on the table and chunks it his way missing him. Glass splatters all over the floor. He laughs sarcastically and opens the door. As he's walking out says, "Bitch, fuck you," and slams the door behind him.

"Janae! What the fuck?" I yell, fixing the spoon on the stove. I turn the pot off with a quick snip, wipe my hands with the dishcloth, and face her arms crossed. I'm livid. Does she know what she's just done? Caused confusion. Confusion between me and Dev that I did not need. Hell, I'm dealing with enough already!

"I did nothing! He did! Within a few months of y'all dating, you have changed into a totally different person!" She says throwing her hands in the air. "I see you are still not going to talk and tell me whats going on. I'm going to fucking bed!" she yells and storms off to her room slamming the door. I throw each hand up screaming to myself, WHAT THE FUCK JUST HAPPENED?! Like seriously! You would think Dev and Nae Nae are the ones in the relationship! One storming out and the other going to their room going to bed! I shake my head. Then rub my temples. Headache city. I turn to the medicine cabinet and grab a bottle of Aleeve. Take three out of the bottle and go to the refrigerator and grab a beer. I need some alcohol. I take my medicine, take a deep breath, and return to cooking. Roughly a couple hours later, six beers and a shot of Grey Goose, my gumbo is done. My poor shrimp are cooked to pieces but the flavor is to savor! I am no longer hungry. Most probably because I don't eat while I drink. Either I eat before, or I may eat after depending on how I'm feeling. I now have a buzz and feel like talking. Janae is going to talk to me. Whether she wants to or not. I walk fast to her room. Faster than I normally would have, but I'm intoxicated, remember? I keep reminding myself too! Haha.

    I knock on her door because I know she's mad. Mad at who? I'm not truly sure, but don't really give a fuck. She doesn't answer. I try the door and it's locked. "Naaae Naae!" I slur. No answer. "Janaaaaaaaeee!" I yell. Still nothing. Is she ignoring me?! I knock harder, then a little harder. Eventually, it turns into a police knock. The fuck is going on?

    "Janae Christian Carter!" I yell. Nothing. "You know what? Fuck you! Just like Dev said when he walked out. FUCK YOU BITCH!" I yell, deciding to leave from by her door. Fuck her. Fucking bitch! What the fuck is she acting like that with me for? I haven't done her shit!

    I fix a double shot. Take it and fix another. "Fuck you!" I yell once more before pouring another shot of Grey Goose. Fuck that bitch! Fuck all this! I wave my hand in the air talking to myself.

    I go take a shower. It took a little bumping into walls, toilets, and sinks before I finally decided one more double shot, and I was done. I'm crying now which lets me know I've had enough. I finish up in the bathroom, somehow, and go to the kitchen to fix the last of the last. I get to the freezer, grab the Grey Goose, and realize I don't know where the fuck the shot glass went. I stand there with the grey goose in hand, trying to make myself remember where I put it. Hmmm… The bathroom counter? No. The tub? No. I don't fucking know. I can't remember. Fuck it. I turn to the cabinet to grab another shot glass and hear the front door screech. It's probably Dev. Fuck him too. I grab my glass, pour my shot, and take it. I stand with my back to the door but hear nothing else. Fuck it. I'm already drunk, one more won't hurt. Then I think about it, yep, I should do another! The motherfucker will be coming in here with some bullshit, and I don't want to hear any of it. I take another shot. MMMM. Well, above my level. I know it and the grey goose probably does too! Haha! I laugh out loud to myself. I hear something fall. I turn. I don't know what it was. I look to my left then to my right. I see nothing. "Who's there?" I say. Maybe I'm being paranoid? Maybe. I grab a knife out of the kitchen drawer and I wait. Nothing. One more shot I guess. I say aloud to myself shrugging my shoulders. "One more," I say, holding up my index finger still talking to myself. I pour one more. I mean why not? I say to myself shrugging my shoulders once again. I don't work tomorrow. I can sleep as late as I want to. All day if I feel like it. Gulp! I swallow the double shot in one swig. I've done became a pro! I laugh to myself. Shit who else can laugh with me? No one else is here. No one else is here! Ugh! I hate this shit! My eyes swell with tears once again. Okay, bedtime. I've reached passed my limit. Time for bed!

Lawd. I take Dramamine like clockwork when I drink, but what the fuck happened last night? See, I have this strange idea that taking something for a headache and Dramamine before bed helps me wake up without a hangover. It normally seems to work or I just don't drink as much as I think I have. Either way, I take it faithfully before bed after any night out. I wake up with a splitting headache and nauseated like a motherfucker! It's been a long time since I've felt like this. I reach over to my nightstand and take two Dramamine. Shit! I have to get up and go get something for a headache too! I say to myself throwing my arms down on the bed in frustration. FUCK! I throw on my robe, go to the kitchen, grab headache medicine and go back to my room. Dev was sitting at the table and Janae was cooking breakfast as she always does. Whoooo, whooo. I take my meds and lay back in my bed. I must be still drunk 'cause I still feel like fuck all this shit.

I wake to the smell of gumbo? Is it really? Mmmm I'm soooo hungry. Then I think about it. I might not be that hungry. I don't feel like facing Dev or Janae right now. Fuck Imma go back to sleep…

As the Dramamine is wearing off, I hear a knock at the door. Ugh! Leave me be! Damn! I'm in my room. Not bothering anyone. Shit!

"Hey, Jazmynn, are you woke?" I hear from the door a voice so familiar. "Uh-uh," I say from under my warm covers.

"Come on, Jazmynn, you slept a whole day away. Get up!" Damn Janae.

"Imma get up in a few," I mumble.

"No. Get up now!" she says, pulling my cover from over my head and completely from off of my body. "Get your ass up right now. Go take you a shower and come to eat that delicious gumbo you cooked." Balling up my cover and throwing it on the floor, I ball up into a ball and pull my pillow over my head hiding my face. This shit is really funny. I feel like a little kid and my mom is waking me and trying to make me get up for school! I start giggling, and then I feel a smack on my ass. "Get up, guh! I hear you giggling. I ain't playing with you!" she says, giggling herself. I peek from under my pillow and locate where she is standing, then pull the pillow from my face and chunk it at her. I aimed directly for her head and SCORE! She stands there in shock with her mouth dropped open. "You little bitch!" She laughs picking it up to throw it back at me. I cross my arms in the air to block her attempt at revenge. She still clocked me on the side of my head. "All right, I'm getting up," I say.

I grab some old blue Hollister warm up joggers out of my drawer and a baby blue tank top then head to the shower. Before I enter I can already smell the scent of Victoria's Secret love spell. I open the door and see a familiar scene. Candles around the tub, soft R&B playing in the background, and wine. I'm not too sure I'm drinking that. Not right now anyway. I glance around the bathroom looking for Dev because I already know it's his work, but there's no sign of him in here nowhere. Oh well, I say to myself. I strip all my clothes off and get in. The water is nice and hot just the way I like it. I lay back, wring my washcloth out and lay the towel over my face. This is soooooo relaxing! My muscles loosen up and I breathe in deeply.

I have the slightest idea how long I was sleeping in the tub, but I guess it wasn't that long, because Janae hadn't come back for me. I grab the bottle of wine and I finally walk to the kitchen to join Janae. She's sitting with an Ebony magazine at the bar eating gumbo and crackers.

"Well, what do ya know? Look who is out of the shower smelling fresh, and is finally out of that bed of hers!" She says to me as I'm walking up. "Yeah, yeah," I say nonchalantly. I grab a bowl out of the cabinet and begin to fix me some gumbo.

"First of all, I wanna apologize for last night. I'm sorry I flew off the handle like that. I just hate to see you hurting or upset. I was way out of line and I apologize. I also apologized to Dev this morning," Janae says turning and facing me. "But do you know he acted like he was surprised? Almost like the motherfucker didn't even know what the fuck I was talking about! I just said, "Well, I'm sorry anyway" and shook my head!

"Damn!" I say. What the fuck is up with him?! I wonder. "It's all good, Nae Nae. I know you are only looking out for my best interest, so I ain't tripping," I say, looking for a spoon in the kitchen drawer.

"So you being sleep and all, I doubt you saw this…" she says, turning the ebony magazine upside down toward me pointing on the page.

Is he single or is he not? Is this a fling or is this a flop?

> *Well, known entrepreneur Peter Williamson looks to have a lady in the picture these days but sources say the relationship may be a little rocky. At a fashion show in New Orleans, Louisiana, a few months back it looked as though he met this mysterious woman while she was attending the show, but other sources say they met previously in Las Vegas, Nevada, some few months before the fashion show. Who is this mystery lady? (Several pictures were plastered all over both sides of the pages of me.*

One at the fashion show, one standing outside of the school with my arms crossed, another from the fashion show in that dress Peter made…)

Sources say she's a counselor at Dillard University which has been verified. (Refer to picture on the right.)

This is why we suspect there may be a few thunderstorms in the air for this couple. This looks like a lovers quarrel. (Pictured below.) Referring to the picture with my arms crossed and some stupid look on my face.

Whatever the case, we at EBONY MAGAZINE hope this is the one for the handsome Williamson. If you or anyone you know has any information on this mystery woman, please email the editor at ebonyeditor2012.mag@yahoo.com. Information must be confirmed factual before payment.

Lovers quarrel? Couple? What are these people talking about? I need to talk to Peter ASAP! "Has Dev seen this?" I whisper.

"Girl, if he hasn't, he will eventually." She pulls two more magazines out of her bag on side of her. One, the *Daily Gossip*, has me and Peter on the front cover with him grabbing me while I had begun to fall while I was on stage captioned "Damsel in distress caught on the runway by bachelor Peter Williamson." And the other with a picture of Peter twirling me modeling the dress he made, saying "Twirl, girl, twirl!" Oh shit, oh shit, oh shit.

"Where's Dev?" I ask Janae.

"In his room," she answers, sipping the juice of her gumbo. I sigh loudly. "What am I going to do?" I whisper to Janae.

"Tell him the truth," she answers plainly.

"I can't do that! He'll never believe the truth with all these pictures circulating all over the media!" I exclaim.

I throw my hands up in frustration. Shake my head. I place my bowl on the counter and just stand there. In walks Dev and Janae quickly closes the magazine and places it on top of the others to not be seen. I look at him placing my hands on my hips.

"Dev, do you remember Peter the owner of that club in Las Vegas?" I ask worriedly of what the outcome will be of this conversation.

"Yeah, why?" he asks, plopping on the couch grabbing the remote turning on the TV.

"Well," I begin. "Remember me and Janae had a girls night a while back? We went to a fashion show and he was there as a guest speaker and there to introduce a new line of clothing he had just invented."

"So?" he asks, completely uninterested.

"Well, he saw us sitting on side of the runway and asked would I model one of his pieces and I said yes." I have his attention now. He turns and faces me in the kitchen now sitting at the edge of the sofa. "So you are just deciding to tell me this now? This has been a few weeks ago, right? When does he want you to model his clothes?" he asks, ending his sentence sarcastically. He's starting to get mad. His nose flares when he's mad and right now it looks like he can smell what I'm thinking.

"Well, see, uh, it was that night. I didn't really think it was a big deal, but now it kind of is. I'm sorry I really am! But the paparazzi took pictures and now have them plastered all over magazines and I don't know where else. I just wanted to tell you about it myself before you saw it in a newspaper or anywhere else but I'm sorry," I say, placing my right hand over my mouth. He now stands and comes into the kitchen.

"You're sorry? You're sorry?! No fucking shit you're sorry!" he yells.

"I know you're upset, but if I knew this all would take place I would've never gone. I'm sorry, I really am," I say, walking toward him with my arms stretched out to hug him, but he pushes my arms aside.

"Do not touch me! You have me walking around here looking stupid! Going to the dude's fashion show and all kind of shit!" he yells.

"It wasn't his fashion show…" I go to say but he cuts me off. "It doesn't fucking matter, Jazmynn! When he asked you to model, you could've said no. You should've said no, Jazmynn!" His face is red as a beet. He is livid. He's right, though. I could've said no. But I wanted to do it!

"You're right, I could've and probably should've, but it seemed like fun! Since when do you care? Any other time you wouldn't give a fuck! I didn't see any harm in it!" I yell back, getting angry myself. Who the fuck does he think he is telling me what I should and shouldn't do?

"We are supposed to be in a relationship, Jazmynn, that's why I care. Where the fuck are the pictures?" he says. I stand silent. He turns to Janae who is sitting front row to the drama. "Where are the pictures? Do you know, Janae?"

She stands, picking up her bowl and empty paper from her crackers. She grabs her magazines and goes to put them back in her bag while saying, "I don't have shit to do with none of this. I don't know about no damn pictures," she answers and mistakenly dropping one. Of course, it had to be one of the ones we are on the cover. He bends over to pick it up, and she does too at the same time making them bump heads. He with his long ass arms manages to grab the magazine first. "What the…" he says, looking at the cover reading the caption. "Damsel in distress." "The fuck is this shit?" he asks, opening to the page of the article. "Looks like you left a good bit out, huh?" he asks, throwing the magazine on the counter. "The fuck is he carrying you for? Where the fuck did he take you? Did you sleep with him? Are you sleeping with him? Is that why you keep turning me down for sex?" he asks. He now has a vein popping out of his neck. He's either going to have a stroke or a heart attack.

"He wasn't carrying me, a guy grabbed my leg and I was about to fall and he caught me. No, I'm not sleeping with Peter," I answer.

"This is some foul shit, Jazmynn," he says, grabbing his coat off the chair walking to the door to leave.

"We need to talk about this, Dev!" I say but he's already out the door.

"Well, that went well," Janae says, sitting back to the bar.

"Ya think?" I answer with a smirk on my face. I mean honestly, it's not a laughing matter, but, I decide to laugh to stop from crying.

Chapter 17

Ugh! Dev hasn't been home in three days. Janae said he's probably at one of his homeboy's house, but I don't know. He won't answer his phone, emails, or text messages. He's completely ignoring me. I'm looking out of the school window as always watching my little twin scurry to her next class. She'll be graduating tomorrow. I'll need to find something else to pass my free time during the long hours I don't put my degree to work. I walk back to my desk and hear a knock at the door.

It's Peter.

"Hello there, beautiful!" he says, entering.

"Hi," I answer shortly.

"Is everything okay?" he asks. "Are you having a bad day or is this bad timing? I can come back some other time." He says walking back to the door.

"I'm fine. It's just… Have you been reading the papers and magazines?"

"I have, that's partially why I'm here. I'm so sorry about that. Honestly, it's beyond my control what they post and write about me, but I wanted to check and see if things were okay on your end."

"Personally, I'm fine. Emotionally and mentally I'm drained. I not long ago was introduced to the gossip and decided to tell Dev before he saw it himself and he went ballistic! He is so pissed at me, and I don't know what to do about it!" I say.

"I apologize for that. I can talk to him if you would like, and let him know there's nothing between us…" he says but I hold a finger up to interject.

"No, that would only make things worse. Hell, the last time you spoke to him you ended up in the hospital for eighteen days. Nah, it's okay. Imma figure it out," I say to him, sort of waiving the conversation away. My reasoning was a little thoughtless, but I feel stuck between a rock and a hard place.

Walking to the window I know one thing I'm going to have to do, and really don't want to, but if I want to try to make this relationship work, I'm going to have to eliminate. "I'm sorry, Peter. I don't think we should see each other anymore." I say quietly. Thinking to myself, is this really what I want to do.

"But, Jazmynn…"

"No buts. I actually feel guilty about going to lunch with you knowing I really like you and want more than friendship. But I'm in a relationship and can't do this. It isn't right nor is it fair to Dev," I say, turning back to face him crossing my arms across my chest.

"Whatever you wish," Peter says, walking up to me hugging me. Damn, damn, damn. Kenneth Cole black. My weakness. Don't lay your head on his shoulder! Don't do it!' I scream to myself, but it's too late. I've already buried my face in his neck drawing in that wonderful smell of cologne.

"What the fuck! Really, Jazmynn?" I hear from the door. We both pull away and look toward the sound of the voice.

Devon. It's fucking Devon. I start walking toward Dev and say, "It's not what you think."

"It's not what I think? It's not what I think?" he repeats. "Well, the fuck is it then?"

Peter steps forward. "Listen, man, I was just leaving. I only came to see how Jazmynn was with all the gossip in the media being that all of it is false. I mean no disrespect, and Jazmynn just told me she doesn't want to see me again and I will respect that."

"Boy, fuck you! You're a bitch and you know exactly what you're doing," Dev says, pointing at Peter's face. I walk around Dev and close my office door. I wonder if I should leave it open for campus security in case things get out of hand?

"Listen, I'm not doing anything. I cannot control what's posted in the media and twisted around for a story. This isn't the first time they have done this and it won't be the last," Peter says, putting his left hand in his pocket holding his right palm up. "Jazmynn and I are just friends. Nothing more."

"Stay your ass away from my girl, Peter," Dev hisses, still pointing at Peter.

"Duly noted." He salutes with his right hand before placing it in his pocket like the left and walking around Dev out of the door. "I don't want you to speak to him ever again!" Dev yelled at me.

Ah-hmm. What?! The hell he thinks he is? I wonder to myself before responding, "I respect how you feel, Devon. But you WILL NOT dictate to me who I can be friends with or not. I'm just letting you know. You said you had let the whole shit go, that you had bigger fish to fry. What's changed? Your ego?" I asked, folding my arms.

"I said what? I don't even talk like that. What the fuck are you talking about, Jazmynn?" he asks, puzzled, then looks like he's seen a ghost thinking. "Well, you need to get your shit together. I'm so sick of this shit!" I yell when I walked out the door slamming it as I left. Wow. I just slammed the door to my own office leaving Dev in it! I decide I'm going to take the rest of the day off, so I go to the office, talk to the dean and leave.

I call Janae and ask her to meet me at Pat O'Brien's bar and head that way. I make it before she does and grab a seat at the bar. The bartender asked, "What will it be pretty lady?" I respond with "The strongest drink you got!"

"It's been that kind of day, eh?" he asks. "I gotcha."

I nod and mouthed thanks.

Janae arrives roughly twenty minutes later.

"What's going on, love? Everything okay?" she asks as she takes a seat beside me.

"Girl," I say, looking at her with an annoyed face. "Tell me why Peter decided to drop by the school today and Dev walked in when he was hugging me bye?"

Her jaw drops. "No!" she says exaggerating the "o."

"Yes!" I say taking another sip of my hand grenade. That bartender is so full of shit! I know he has a stronger drink than this!

"He told Peter to stay his ass away from me which I had already told Peter I could no longer see him. But when Peter left, I made sure to tell Dev bitch-ass he can't tell me who I can be friends with and who I can't."

"Good for you. The motherfucker has his nerves!" she said, rolling her eyes. "And if I were you, I wouldn't quit talking to Peter and being his friend. He's a cool dude and very sweet."

"I know, but, Nae Nae," I turn toward her. "I like him a lot. Like a lot, lot," I say.

"I know, and that's okay! You aren't married to Dev and you're young. You have a lot of life to go. You don't have to settle with one person until you are ready and decide that's what you want to do. Your happiness is all that matters, and if you're happy, I'm happy! Now, let's drink and be merry!" she lifts her glass to toast. I laugh. She always knows exactly what to say, how to say it, and when to say it. She's totally right.

Vroom, vroom, my cell phone vibrates under my pillow. I reach under and grab it to read the message.

"I'm sorry about the other day. Had I known your boyfriend was coming, I would not have intruded. I won't call or text you anymore, I promise. But I felt I really needed to apologize for any confusion I may have caused. Have a wonderful day, beautiful."

Peter. He has been on my mind since the day I met him. Now I'm not supposed to talk to him or be friends with him. Fuck that! Nothing has changed with me and Dev. It's still the same old shit. I gave him some the night that crap happened and it's like he's forgotten all about everything with Peter. We are still in the tabloids, but it's not as bad as before. Most of them now title "Trouble in paradise" and shit like, "Where has the mystery woman gone?" I laugh aloud to myself. I'm right here! Haha. I decide I will text back. Hell, I will text and ask what he's doing!

"You are very sweet. Thanks. You don't have to stop calling or texting, I can't see myself being an asshole and stopping a friendship because of an idiot. Are you down for breakfast?" (I look at the alarm clock on my nightstand, six thirty.) What you say about eight at Biscuits and buns on bank?'

Say yes. Say yes. Say yes! I scream inwardly.

"Sure."

"Awesome!" I jump up grabbing under clothes and my robe to run and take a shower. I grab the handle to open the door, but it's locked. Who is up this early on a Saturday? Knock, knock!

"Hold up! Shit!" says Dev, sounding angry. Shit. "Okay," I answer, thinking of a quick lie. I already know he's going to ask me where I'm going so early on a Saturday without Janae. Okay, I got it! I'm tutoring!

He opens the door wrapped in a towel. Damn. That's why I'm still with him. He is fucking sexy.

"What are you doing up so early?" Dev asked with an attitude.

"Well, what are you doing up so early?" I ask, placing my clothes on the bathroom counter.

"I'm going job hunting," he says nonchalantly.

"On a Saturday?" I ask. That's dumb. Who goes job hunting on a Saturday? Why is he job hunting anyway? He has a job at Coscos!

"Yeah, well, I need a job, don't I?" He looks at me and asks raising his right eyebrow. "And what are you doing up so early?" he asks.

"I have a student that needs a little extra help for one of her classes and I told her I would help, so I'm meeting her at a coffee shop to see what I can help her with," I answer. I'm such a horrible liar. I'm sooooo hoping he doesn't realize I'm up to no good. I chuckle. Shit!

"Oh, okay." That's all he says. Oh, okay. Does he even give a damn?!

I start the shower and begin to undress while he is in the mirror shaving. I bend over to remove my panties and he flies behind me. Poking me with his bulge through his towel. We all know what time it is. The bad part is I am actually a little horny. I pop my ass on him a little bit, making it ripple. That's all it takes for his towel to fall to the floor. The bathroom is getting fogged with the heat from the shower. I stand allowing him to grab at my breasts slowly kissing my neck. He rubs his hands up and down my body and it's so sensual. So pleasurable, but so repetitive. It's the same shit every fucking time. I'm so hot that it's actually not bothering me to realize that. Then again, the more I think about it, it is. Sigh. What time is it? I reach over to the counter and grab my phone. Seven ten. Ah-ah, oh no. Sorry, buddy. No time today. I sit my phone back on the counter and turn facing him. "Sorry, baby, I need to get ready to go." Kiss him on the lips and turn back to the shower door and enter. He stands there shock. Naked and shocked. I let the water run down my face and through my hair. Grab some shampoo and lather my hair. Rinse then condition. I then grab my shower gel and put some on my loofah. My eyes are closed to be sure not to get any soap or conditioner in my eyes and feel a draft. I try to open my eyes and it begins to burn. I wince and closed them tighter. I feel hands on my ass. Very light. Squeezing a little here and there. Then I feel the body behind me and get poked in the back with his rod. Wow. Really, Dev? He then pushes the top of my back physically telling me to bend over.

"No, Dev, I have to go," I say to him, standing straight as a board.

"Yes," he demands. Pushing the top of my back once again a little more forcefully.

"I said no, Devon. I'm not in the mood," I insist.

Before I know it, he grabs the back of my neck and forces it toward the floor to bend me down. I am now pissed. The fuck is he doing? I swing my fist behind me hoping to connect. "Stop it, Dev, I'm not playing," I say now under the shower of water, eyes full of soap and on fire.

"You thought this was a game? You think you can just tease me like that and do nothing and get away with it? Bitch, please! Bend over and shut the fuck up. You better not wake Janae either!" he demands in a voice I've never heard before.

"You're hurting me!" I scream, attempting to turn my body around in confusion.

He pulls my head back using a handful of hair and whispers in my ear, "Shut the fuck up, bitch, and do what the fuck I said."

The fuck?! I swing my right arm toward my back and this time he grabs it. I swing with the left, and he grabs that one too. I attempt to turn around again, but the way he has my arms it hurts and I still can't fucking see! "FUCKING STOP IT, DEV!" I yell angrily twisting and trying to break loose of his grasp. He grabs my hair once again, this time almost making my head touch my ass while holding both wrists with his other hand. "Bitch, I said shut the fuck up. Bend the fuck over." Is he fucking serious right now?

"Are you kidding me right now? So you're that guy? I don't want to have sex so you're going to take it? GET OFF ME!" I scream attempting once more to free myself. Before I know it He slaps me on my right side of my face. Hard. Ouch! "Shut up, bitch!" he hisses and inserts himself where it doesn't go.

"Aiiieeee!" I scream in pain. I try to stand straight but it hurts back there, I can't move my arms, and he's squeezing the shit out of my neck which he is holding firmly down. He thrusts himself into me with a force from hell. "Dev, stop, please! You're hurting me!" I beg.

"Uh! Mhm!" he moans.

"Please, Devon, stop!" It gets worse each stroke. I begin to cry. I honestly don't believe this shit. He is raping me! His fucking girlfriend!

"Yeah, bitch! Ugh! Ugh! UUUUgh!" He releases in no time and finally pulls himself out of me. Although it was quick, the pain felt like an eternity. The water is now running cold. He finally releases his hold on my neck and wrists, shoves me toward the wall making me fall face first into it and backs off. I brace myself by putting my hands in front of me on the shower wall. The pain is excruciating. Worst that my cycle cramps. My behind burns and feels like it's a foot wide. I see blood running down my legs being washed away with water. I fall to my knees in tears. I hear him leave out of the bathroom and feel relieved. I tell myself, man up. I attempt to quickly bathe so I can get out of this cold ass shower, but I scrub and scrub and still don't feel clean. Fucking bastard. That fucking bastard.

I'm a whole hour late meeting Peter because of trying to cover the red hand impression on the right side of my face and the knot coming on my forehead. As soon as I walk up, I begin to apologize. "I am so sorry for my tardiness. I got caught up at home. I would've been here on time, but…" I cannot tell him what just happened. I mean he's my friend, but that's too personal. Why would Dev do that to me? I start crying uncontrollably. I'm still hurting. Peter stands up and extends his left hand.

"Come, Jazmynn. You're too beautiful to be crying, and crying in public. Let me take you somewhere private." I grab his hand, and we exit the diner. Once we enter his car, he tells his driver to bring him to his townhouse. He grabs me and puts me under his left arm and hugs me with his right. He doesn't say a word. He just holds me tight. Making me feel safe. We arrive at his home and I've finally stopped crying, but I know I look a mess. My eyes feel swollen, my face is sticky from tears, and I'm beyond embarrassed. He helps me up the steps and into his extravagant home. It is gorgeous! We are greeted at the door by a housekeeper. She looks shocked. I don't know if it's shocked to see me because of the tabloids or shocked because he never brings women home.

"Get the spa team together, Catalyna, have Rouel make breakfast, and hold all calls until further notice please," he says to her and gently guides me up the stairs. We enter a room that's completely dark then he claps his hands twice and the lights come on. This dude has a fucking movie theater in his home! There's a big screen projector on the wall and several fancy reclining chairs in a row, with a huge sofa right behind them. "Have a seat," Peter says and I sit on the couch. The couch is so big, my feet don't even touch the floor. I kick off my shoes, grab the throw blanket that was laying on one of the arms, and sit Indian style wrapping myself in the soft blanket.

Peter sits beside me opening his arms for me to move closer and lay on his chest. I begin to cry once more. I'm still hurting.

"Do you want to talk about it?" he asks. "If you don't, it's fine. We can sit here as long as you want, I'm at your disposal." I take a deep breath. I really do need to let this out. My heart hurts, and my body does as well. I sit up facing Peter, but before I could start, he asks, "Jazmynn! What happened to your face?!" He touches my cheek softly. "Hold on," he says getting up grabbing the remote control for the TV off of the end table. He turns it on and presses a couple buttons and a man's face appears on the screen. "Jacob, Have Catalina bring up an ice pack, please."

"Yes, sir," he answers and the screen turns black once again.

Turning back to me, looking sympathetic, "What happened sweetheart? Who did this?" he asks, sitting back down on side of me.

I had stopped crying, but my eyes begin to swell with tears once again.

It takes everything I have in me to actually be able to say the words aloud, but I finally muster the strength. "Dev raped me," I eventually say, bursting into tears once again.

"He WHAT?" Peter asks in shock.

"I-I told him, no, and he-he wouldn't stop! I know it may sound crazy being he is my boyfriend and all, but I begged him to stop! My face is like this because he slapped me and told me to shut the fuck up, and pushed me against the shower wall when he was done," I say with my hands covering my face.

"Did you call the police?" Peter asks.

"No," I answer between tears. "I showered and left to come to meet you. I'm so scared of what he might do. I didn't think I would turn into this emotional wreck, but I'm hurt. Mentally, physically, and emotionally. I can't believe he did this to me!" I say through tears.

"You should call the police and file a report. Get a restraining order against him too. That sick bastard! Where is he now?" Peter asks, looking like he's pissed.

"I don't know," I say. "He just finished and left."

"I'll find him!" Peter says, standing to his feet. "Don't you worry! He will never do anything like that to you again!"

"What are you going to do, Peter?" I ask, now scared. Does Peter not remember his hospital stay? Who knows what Devon will do to him if he tries to confront him?

"I will make him wish he never met you! Jazmynn, a man should never put his hands on a woman unless she wants him to, and I mean that in a good way. That sick, sorry bastard!" he says, pacing the floor. "Besides that, when a woman says no, the fucking answer is no! Girlfriend, wife, whoever!" Peter says angrily while now walking toward the door. "The spa staff will be in here shortly. Make yourself comfortable and be treated as a real woman should. I'm stepping out for a moment. Won't be gone long." He blows me a kiss and exits through the door.

Six ladies dressed in white T-shirts and black tights enter. One hands me a robe and tells me to go to the restroom and put it on, pointing to the north of the room. They all smile sweetly at me and seem friendly. I don't know if it's sincere or if they are just doing their job. I come out of the restroom in the robe and notice they have switched the movie room into a sort of a spa. There's a table for me to lay on, a chair for a pedicure, and another chair with a vanity mirror. Wow! I could get used to this. I'm instructed to remove my robe and lie in a supine position on the table. They cover me with a sheet. One girl places eucalyptus soaked cucumbers on my eyes and instructs me to relax. I have twelve sets of hands on my body at once. One applying some kind of scream to my face that smells like bananas, two on each side each with an arm and leg apiece, and one on my feet rubbing one, then doing the same to the other.

I'm almost sleeping when one of the girls uncovers my eyes, dries my face, and tells me to turn over. They begin to massage my back, shoulders, and legs making me feel like I'm turning into jelly. They are rubbing my muscles hard, not too hard but just hard enough.

I fall asleep.

I'm awakened by Catalyna. "Ma'am, it's almost lunchtime and you haven't touched your breakfast. Is it of your liking? Would you like something else prepared?" I sit up on the table grabbing the sheet around me looking around for the robe I had on earlier. Catalyna walks over handing it to me from off the back of a chair then turns her back to me giving me the privacy to put it on.

"No, ma'am. I'm not hungry," I answer in a low voice now covered. She turns back to face me and says, "Ms. Jazmynn, Mr. Williamson gave me strict instructions to make sure you eat. You should try to eat something. Anything you want the chef will cook to order."

"But I'm not…" I go to say being cut off. "I'm not taking no for an answer." She sounds like a mom. "How about a fried shrimp po'boy with a sliced pickle and some homemade french fries? Boy oh boy, that's the chef's specialty. Talk about good!" she says, attempting to cheer me up.

"I like shrimp," I say, cracking a smile.

"Shrimp it is, Ms. Jazmynn, coming right up!" And she leaves out heading to the kitchen to put in my food order. A moment later the six spa women walk in again. The leader (well, I'm guessing she's the leader because she's the only one who always talks) asks if I'm ready to continue my spa treatment. "Uh, yes, I guess," I answer unsure of what's to come. If they are planning on giving me more of that massage, I just hope they know I'm going to fall asleep again!

"Sit here," she says, pointing to the pedicure chair. Once seated I have two women beginning a pedicure on each foot and two with each a hand. Another begins brushing my hair, and the leader stands supervising. She grabs the TV remote and turns on soft music. I'm getting sleepy once again. I sit with my eyes closed knowing they are all staring at my face, but I'm so relaxed I don't care. The girl brushing my hair is so gentle. Here and there her soft hands brush across my forehead collecting my hair as she brushes.

In walks Catalyna with a covered tray. Must be my food. I've actually gained an appetite while waiting for it to be cooked and delivered. The spa women begin to pack up all of their items and the leader tells me they will be back later for makeup. Catalyna uncovers the dish and it looks amazing. I have the po'boy and fries and an extra cup of fried shrimp.

"You're in for a treat, Ms. Jazmynn," she says while pulling a tray up from the side of the chair I'm sitting in and placing the food in front of me. "Enjoy," she says sweetly before walking out giving me privacy to eat. She never asked me what I wanted to drink, I say to myself noticing the water with lemon she brought. That's exactly what I wanted!

The food is delicious, and although I can't finish the fries, I eat every bit of the po'boy and the extra shrimp. He put his foot in this! I slide my tray toward the side of the chair and recline it a little. Ate my belly full, now I'm sleepy again! Awe, shit, now I have to pee. I get up out of my comfortable position and go to the bathroom.

After finishing, I look at myself in the mirror. My skin glows. I still have a red imprint on my face, and the knot on my forehead, but it's not as bad as it was. The bags under my eyes from crying are gone and I look refreshed. My behind still hurts, though. As I sat to pee I notice blood in my panties. I start to tear up as I wipe realizing I need another bath and an extra change of clothes. I flush and wash my hands, then I walk back to sit and decide to plop on the couch. It'll be waaay more comfortable if I go back to sleep. I sit and feel a vibration under the throw cover. Vrmm. Vrmm.

It's a text on my cell. Thirty-three missed calls, seventeen voicemails, and fifteen text messages.

Devon: Where are you?

What are you doing?

I'm sorry about this morning. Let me make it up to you.

Answer your fucking phone!

You out fucking some other dude now?

I'm sorry, baby, I'm just worried about where you are.

Are you okay?

Why the fuck are you ignoring me? I told you I was fucking sorry.

Fuck you, bitch!

You're a fucking hoe anyway.

ANSWER YOUR MOTHERFUCKING PHONE AND IM NOT PLAYING WITH YOU, JAZMYNN.

I didn't mean to hurt you. I would never hurt you.

I love you.

Stop fucking ignoring me.

Where the fuck you at? And don't lie, because I already know you're not with Janae.

He is blowing my phone up! What an asshole! He loves me in one message, and fuck me in the other? I text back, "Leave me the fuck alone. It's none of your business where I am. You will never find me and if you ever try to do that shit to me again. I WILL KILL YOU, you sick bastard!"

I call Janae, but get her voicemail. I leave the message for her to call me ASAP; it's important. My phone vibrates again. Vrmm vrmm.

Devon: "We'll see about that, hoe…"

I, for the life of me, don't know how I could have fallen in love with this person. I mean he never came off the type to disrespect women like this let alone put his hands on one! Peter walks in with flowers and a gift bag.

"I know this by no way can make you feel better, but I do want you to know on behalf of all REAL men, I apologize for your boyfriends' actions."

"Ex-boyfriend," I interject.

"Well, ex-boyfriend," he says with a little smile. He hands me the bouquet, I smell them and mumble, mmm. He smiles with satisfaction then hands me the bag.

"Thank you, Peter, I appreciate this. I love flowers!" I say, opening the gift bag. I pull out a small black case saying Beretta and open it. It looks like a flashlight, but I can't figure out how to turn it on. What the hell did he buy me a flashlight for?

"Here like this," he says taking it from my hand and making it make a clacking noise. "It's a Baretta Taser for your protection. It's small for the convenience of carrying it in your pocket daily. Try it," he says, handing it back to me. I press the small button on the side of it and Claaaack! It goes sharing electricity between two posts. I smile in excitement. I really like it.

"Thank you, Peter! I feel safer already!" I open my arms, throwing myself between his for a hug.

"Catalyna told me she got you to eat. Shrimp, eh? Haha!" he laughs.

Letting go of my embrace, I take a step back and look up at his face. "Devon has been blowing my phone up," I say like a little kid telling on another.

"He has, eh? Don't worry about him he will be dealt with soon enough," Peter answers confidently. I wonder what he means by that.

Ring, ring! My phone rings, its Janae.

"Hello?"

Janae: "Hey, girl, where you at?" Her voice sounds desperate.

"I'm at Peter's house, I've been trying to call you. Ask her where that motherfucker lives, tell her you want to go meet her, and you better make that shit sound real too!" I hear a voice whispering to her.

Janae" "Wh-where he lives at? I want to come to meet you." She sounds scared.

"Are you okay? Is Devon there?" I ask.

Janae: "Uh, no. No, I don't know where that is, oh, yes okay, I understand." Oh my God! Dev's holding her hostage! What if he tries to rape her too? "Hold on one second, Janae, one second."

Janae: "Hurry!" I can hear the desperation in her voice. "Hu-hurry, girl, I ain't got all day to wait for no directions."

I turn to Peter. Eyes wide with terror. "What's wrong, is that him?" he asks, holding his hand out for the phone. I shake my head no. "It's Janae. I think he has her hostage. He wants to know where you live to come to get me I guess," I say scared out of my wits.

Peter calls out to Janae as I turn the speakerphone on.

Janae: "Uh, yes?"

"The address is 2024 Rampart Drive," he bellows out.

Janae: "Okay, thanks."

As she goes to hang up, we hear in the background a voice this time well above a whisper.

"This motherfucker thinks he bad, huh? 2024 Rampart Drive? We gone see just how bad he is. That motherfucker was told good to stay away from Jazmynn, and he got the nerve to have her at his house, and gonna give you the address to go meet them? Awe, fuck nah!" Click!

The phone hangs up.

"What are we going to do if he really does come here?" I ask, full of concern while trembling with terror. The whole situation is not going to end well. I feel it.

"Maybe I should just leave. If he comes and finds out I'm not here, he will probably leave and just go out looking for me around town," I say that out loud but mainly to myself. I should dress. Peter walks over to his bar and pours himself a shot and drinks it. I walk to the bathroom to dress, but my clothes are gone. "Where are my belongings?" I ask Peter.

"The maid probably took them to wash them, be right back," and he leaves out. This time, I decide to follow and explore the house that I will never probably see again. I put my taser in the pocket of the robe and walk out of the theater room. I look over the balcony to see Peter talking to one of his security guards.

"Everyone be on the lookout. He may be combative and may not, but just be aware, 'cause I know he's coming. Hell, I would run through the gates of hell for her too."

The balcony screeches from me leaning on it and he looks up at me. I hurry and step back not to be seen. I notice a window overlooking the backyard. The scene is so beautiful and colorful. The whole backyard is full of flowers and trees with a fountain in the middle. There are lounge chairs to the east, west, and under the trees. It is amazing looking across the backyard at this beautiful scenery. I begin to feel a calmness and peace of mind take over.

"Here," I hear from behind. "Your clothes aren't completely dry, this is all I have if you would still like to change." He hands me a T-shirt and some Nichols State University warm-ups. They are going to fit me a little baggie, but I still decide to put them on.

"Thanks," I say, hurrying back into the theater room.

"Jazmynn," Peter stops me. "You do know you don't have to spend all your stay in that room, right?" he asks laughing.

"Well, I, uh," I said, shrugging my shoulders. "Get dressed and I can give you a tour," he says, still laughing.

Devon didn't come yesterday, and I can't help but wonder how Janae is. She hasn't answered the phone or texted me back. Peter has been a complete gentleman with no kind of sexual advances or any kind of bullshit. He held me most of the night and kept me comfortable, safe, and happy. We watched at least three movies before I passed out in his arms. He carried me to his bed, tucked me under the covers, and locked the door on his way out. Big as this house is, I guess he slept in one of the guest rooms.

I get up and the phone in the room rings. *Thuuur, thuuur!* I go to answer it, but remember I'm a guest and decide to leave it be. It rings a couple more times before stopping. I go to the bathroom and notice I have a brandnew toothbrush laying on the counter for me.

How sweet and thoughtful. I brush my teeth and wash my face and head downstairs.

To my right is Peter's study/library. I stand in the doorway admiring the huge collection of books he has.

"Good morning, beautiful," I hear from behind. I turn to see Peter shirtless with white basketball shorts and house slippers.

"Good morning," I answer back sweetly. "I was wondering, would you bring me by my home to check on Janae? She hasn't answered any calls or text messages since we talked to her. I'm worried about her. I also need a shower," I ask.

"Sure can do, you can grab some clothes too." He looks at me from head to toe. "Because I need them warm-ups back, they're my favorite." He snickers, putting one hand over his mouth with the other on his hip. "Although you do wear them a little better than I do." He points, referring to the bottom of my legs. I have one pulled up to my calf and the other all the way down.

"Haha, very funny," I say, giggling.

Chapter 18

We head to my house in Peter's expedition with four bodyguards. I'm so nervous, I can feel like I can vomit the breakfast I was not long finished eating on cue. I take deep breaths all the way there. Man. What if Dev is there waiting for me to come in the house? What if he's done something to Janae? Deep down, I wish these thoughts would go away because I feel like Dev wouldn't hurt Janae. Or would he? I didn't think he would hurt me and here I am, hurt and shit. My behind finally feels better, but I still feel so filthy.

We pull up and I notice Dev's car is gone. Phew! Now to get in, check on Janae, and grab some clothes before he pops up. We get out and walk to the door. Two of the bodyguards guard the door and the other two comes inside with us. The house reeks. Like really bad. Sort of like rotting meat.

"Janae?" I say, covering my nose to attempt to muffle the smell. I turn on the living room light and round the corner heading to Janae's bedroom. One of the bodyguards stood by the door and the other and Peter followed me to Janae's room. I tried to open the door but it was locked. Knock, knock! "Janae! It's me Jazmynn, open up!" No answer. I put my ear to the door to try to hear if I can hear any movement. Nothing. I knock harder this time making the door rattle each hit. It doesn't usually do that. Peter can tell I'm getting extremely concerned. He grabs my arm and stops me from knocking. Looks at the bodyguard and points at the door not saying a word. He pulls me back to allow the guard to place himself center with the door. Donk!

Donk! He kicks the door with a thud. It doesn't budge just rattles. He then takes a step back and runs into the door with his shoulder. OOMPH! He grunts and the door cracks open a little. Something is blocking the door. I take a step forward to see if I can fit through the crack, but it's not quite wide enough. I step back once again to let him hit it again. This time he hits it and flies into the room almost as if nothing were behind the door blocking it. He must have gotten mad, 'cause the force of that last hit came out of nowhere.

We walk into Janae's room and her room is upside down. Looks like there was some sort of struggle. Her clothes are thrown all over the room scattered across the bed, on the lampshade, even on her windowsill and the window is wide open. I notice a necklace I bought her last Christmas that said "Best friends" with half a heart (because I have the other half) was on the floor broken. I bend to pick it up, but Peter stops me. "We need to call the police, Jazmynn," he says with his eyes full of tears.

"Wha-yhy?" I ask with my eyes wide with terror.

"Janae, she's… she's…" he starts.

"She's what?" I yell. "Spit it out!" I say, throwing my arms in a whirl.

"She's gone," he says, looking manly but trying to hold back tears.

"What do you mean, gone?" I say, tears now swelling in my eyes. He points to Janae's bathroom. I run in and scream. Argh! I run over to her. She is wedged between the toilet and the bathtub in a pool of blood. I pull her left leg, gently sliding her to the middle of the floor and check her pulse. I can't even see her through the blur of my tears. She's lying on her side. I feel nothing and she's cool and sweaty. I turn her on her back and begin to do CPR. I pump her chest, breathe, pump her chest, and breathe. I check for a pulse. Nothing. Peter comes from behind me, grabbing me to make me stop and I yell, "NO! Call an ambulance!" and begin CPR again. This time she gasps and begins to vomit, coughing up blood. I hurry and turn her to her right side so she doesn't aspirate. She starts mumbling something inaudible.

"Hush," I say. "I'm right here. Just hold on, help is coming."

Peter returns to the bathroom telling me an ambulance is in route. I grab a big towel off of the rack and clean Janae's face. Then sit beside her rubbing her back telling her everything will be okay. I keep trying to convince her she needs to keep her eyes open, but she keeps going in and out. I use the towel to clean the floor where she vomited. I can hear the ambulance pulling up outside and whisper to Janae, "They're here!" and at that moment, realize she's not breathing again. I flip her on her back and start CPR again. The ambulance drivers come in and relieve me and start resuscitating her. She gasps once more. "Thank you, God," I whisper silently. They put her on the stretcher and take her out. I ride in the ambulance with her and Peter and the guards follow.

She flat lines two more times before reaching the hospital.

The doctor comes out after ten long hours of waiting in the waiting room. Janae has four broken ribs, which punctured her lungs, she has a bullet lodged in her heart and severe internal bleeding. She was also overdosed on painkillers so they had to pump her stomach. The doctor said she needed immediate surgery and there was a chance she would not make it out, but, with all the internal bleeding and the location of the bullet; she wouldn't make it much longer without it. There was a fifty-fifty chance of recovery. He warned us the police had been notified because although she may have overdosed herself with the painkillers, the gunshot wound was in no way self-inflicted.

Two police detectives show up at the hospital looking at everyone in their paths as if they were suspects. They talk to the doctor that talked to us for a while, and then one of the bodyguards point out that the doctor is pointing at us. A few minutes later, the detectives come up to us.

Extending her right hand, "Good afternoon, I'm Detective Lyneye"—pointing to the other officer—"and this is Detective Prejean. We were told by the doctor you guys brought the young lady in. Can you tell us who she is?" she asks.

"Her name is Janae Christian Carter," I answer.

"And what is your relationship to Ms. Carter?" Detective Prejean asks.

"We are roommates and best friends," I say.

"Okay. Would you know her age?" asks Detective Lyneye.

"She's twenty-three."

"Do you know her date of birth?" asks Detective Prejean.

"January 20, 1989," I answer once again.

"What about her social?" Detective Prejean asks with a smirk.

"Uh, nooo… I—" I go get ready to say being cut off by Detective Lyneye.

"That was rhetorical. He's just trying to lighten the mood." She elbows him and looks at him with a stern face. "How long have you known Ms. Carter?" she asks.

"About five years, going on six now," I say. I begin to think about when we met. I was in the park working on a poem I was writing sitting on a park bench and she came to sit beside me. At first, she glanced and turned her nose up at me never saying a word. Then I noticed three loud girls walking not far from us laughing and playing around. She (Janae) turned to me and asked, "Can you please pretend to be my friend? These girls pick a fight with me every day about the fact that I don't have friends. I'm honestly not in the mood today to fight, and I kinda don't, but can you please help me?" I looked shocked. Like, why doesn't this gorgeous girl not have friends? Who wouldn't want to be friends with her?

"Oookkkay," I say, starting to giggle. "I'm not quite sure what I'm supposed to do?" I say, still giggling. "I laugh when I'm nervous or put on the spot," I tell Janae.

"Girl, you doing well, look at them watching us," she says, giggling.

"What's your name?" I ask, moving to sit closer to her.

"Janae. Juh-nae," she says. I'm guessing not many people pronounce her name correctly for the enunciation.

"Mine is Jazmynn," I say back. "J-A-Z-M-Y-N-N," I spell out.

"Dang! A whole spelling lesson, huh?" Janae asks.

"Well, hell, you gave an enunciation lesson!" We both laugh hysterically. The other girls are bored with our show and start to walk away.

"Hey, thanks," Janae says, noticing their loss of interest.

"Sure," I say back to her. We sit in silence for a few minutes. Occasionally looking each other way giving a friendly smile.

"You know, I don't have many friends myself, I'm sort of a loner," I say, attempting to start a conversation.

"Well, I got friends. A lot of them, they just, you know, busy," Janae says back, sounding unconvincing.

"Okay, cool, well, if you ever just want to hang out." I write my number on a small piece of paper and hand it to her. "Give me a ring." I pack up my things to go but before leaving turn and say, "It was nice to meet you Juh-Nae!"

"You too," she answered, grinning. From that day on, we were inseparable. Until tonight. I'm not allowed to see her yet and it's taking everything I have in me not to lose it.

"Ms. Jazmynn, do you know anyone who would wish harm upon or who would try to hurt Ms. Carter?"

I put my head down. Do I say Dev was the last person to be around her? I really don't know for certain. Shit. I need to say something fast. "Well, our roommate Dev…" I begin to say being cut off by Detective Prejean.

"You have another roommate? Name please!" he demands. He seems like he got a little upset like I was withholding information but they are the ones asking the questions. I'm just answering what I'm asked!

"Yes, we did, well, I mean we do," I say.

"And what is this person's name?" asks Detective Lyneye.

"Devon Edward Thomas," I answer remembering the previous questions about Janae. "He's twenty-two. Born March 15, 1990. No, I don't know his social security number." I smile sarcastically at Detective Prejean.

"And what's your relationship to him?" asks Prejean, ignoring my sarcasm.

"He's… He's my… My ex-boyfriend," I say, stuttering.

"Ex?" asks Prejean.

"Yes, EX." I sneer.

Detective Lyneye elbows Prejean as a hint to stop.

"Why is he your ex, Ms. Barkley?" asks Detective Lyneye as if she really cared.

I look back at Peter. He sighs, shaking his head in disappointment. Then nods for me to tell them.

Tears begin to once again swell in my eyes. How many times will I have to retell this story and keep reliving what happened? I rather pretend it never happened!

"Uhm, he raped me yesterday morning," I finally answer in a small voice. I feel empty. I'm lost and confused. Why in the world would he do something like that to me and I would give it to him every time he wanted! I've never refused him! Lord knows I've faked so many times hoping he would go ahead and get it over with!

"Have you filed a report?" asks Detective Prejean.

"No," I answered, beginning to drown myself in tears. Peter comes over to console me by putting his arms around me guiding my head to his chest.

"Ma'am, if what you are saying is true, charges can be filed against Mr. Thomas, but you will have to submit a statement," says Detective Lyneye. Now she looks concerned. Almost as if she can relate. "Ma'am, a lot of women figure they are in a relationship so the guy will get off scot-free, but that is not the case. If you said no, the answer is no. Rape is rape whether you are in a relationship or not. Let's have the doctors do a rape kit on you. Have you bathed?"

My sobs have eased up and I look at her. "He raped me in the shower. Yes, I've bathed. At least ten times since it has happened, and I still feel I can't get his smell off me!" I say between sobs. Peter stands and walks back over to his bodyguards whispering something to them.

"Do you want to press charges against him?" asks Detective Lyneye.

I stare at her for a few minutes. I look back at where Peter is. I need to press charges, don't I? Like, isn't that the right thing to do? But what if we go to court and he tells them I encouraged it? That it was I who enticed him? What if the judge actually believes I led him on? I can't deal with this anymore. Hopefully, he never comes back around and I can live the rest of my life in peace!

"No, ma'am," I answer avoiding her eyes. I know they are like daggers waiting to stab me in my eyes once our eyes make contact.

She takes a deep breath and exhales, "Do you have somewhere to stay until the investigation of your home is complete?" asks Detective Lyneye. I glance back again and then to the detectives. Peter steps forward. "Are you okay?" he asks. "Yes, um, would it be okay for me to stay with you a couple days until they are done investigating at my house? I won't be a bother. I promise. I will probably stay up here most of the time anyway," I ask.

"Yes. You're more than welcome," he answers.

Turning back to the detectives, "Yes I have somewhere else to stay, but can I go get clothes?" I ask.

"I'm sorry, but at the present moment no. As soon as we are done investigating your home we can contact you and let you know it's clear," Prejean says, shaking his head no.

I sigh. "Okay, thanks. Please let me know anything you guys find out about who did this to her please!" I plead.

A day of trying to sleep in the waiting room of the hospital, they finally put Janae in the intensive care unit and allow me to see her. She's in a coma, looks horrible, and is still barely breathing. She's plugged to all kind of machines and the noise is unbearable. Peter has been up to see me about three times pleading with me to come to get rest and eat, but I can't make myself leave Janae's side. What if she wakes up and I'm not here? I have to be here for her. Just like she was for me. When she wakes up, my face will be the one she sees first; not a nurse. I refuse to have her have to ask where I am. We are besties for life… No, sisters…

BEEEEEEEEEEEEEEEEEEEEEEEEEEEEEEEEEEEEEEEE EEEEEEEEEEEEEEEEEP! A machine goes off. I wake up frantic. I hadn't even realized I had fallen asleep! I look around the room remembering where I am and notice her life support machine has flat-lined. "Help!" I yell. "Help! She's unresponsive!" I run to the door screaming. "Somebody! Anybody! NURSE!" A bunch of people come from all over and push past me in the room. They start to resuscitate her and I'm standing there in total shock. COME ON, JANAE, I scream inside. She can't leave me! No, not now! I'm so scared! As tears began to roll out of my eyes I begin to pray. I pray this isn't the end for her. I pray it's not her time. I pray she makes it out of here. What will I do without her?!

Peter shows up once again while I'm sitting in the waiting area this time with food. They've made me leave the room, but told me roughly fifteen minutes ago she was stabilized. I don't know how much more of this I can deal with! I want my friend back. My sister. I need her! I don't have an appetite but I know I need to eat something. I haven't eaten since Peter's chef made me that poboy.

"Is everything all right?" asks Peter, looking around the waiting room. "Why are you out here and not in the room with Janae?"

"She flat-lined about thirty-five minutes ago, and they made me leave. They came about fifteen minutes ago and said she was stable, though," I answer weakly. I am burnt out. Tired, sleepy, and stressed.

"Man, I hate that," Peter says handing me the brown paper bag of food he brought for me. "Here, please eat this," he says. "I know you may not have an appetite, but you need to try to eat something and put something on your stomach. You won't be any good to Janae if you end up getting sick from not eating," he says while grabbing the seat next to me. "It's my chef's famous chicken salad. He fixed a sandwich and also put a bowl of it with saltine crackers in case you don't eat it on bread."

"Mhmm," I moan. "Don't sound too bad!" I open the bag and begin to lay out all that was in it. Once I opened the bowl of chicken salad and smelled the aroma, it was all over! My appetite was back. I realized I was starving!

"I don't know!" I answer in tears. Several different people have been in here asking me who shot Janae, and the motherfuckers act like I'm the one who did it! I have told them a million times I wasn't at the fucking house I was at Peter's! Shit! The fuck is really going on? I am at a total loss.

Detective Prejuen said, "Yeah, you know, and you probably in on it. What are you getting out of this? Are you that fucked up in the head?" he says, holding both hands on both sides of his head. "Your best bet is to talk. 'Cause when we catch up with Mr. Devon all plea bargains are out the door. Where the FUCK is he?"

"I don't know! We aren't together anymore! I already told you!" I scream.

"Oh yeah, he raped you. Your boyfriend raped you and he tried to kill your friend..." he says.

I think about what Janae would do in this predicament. Lawyer. "Am I a suspect? Am I being detained?"

"Yes, ma'am, you are," answered Detective Prejean.

"UM... well, I need my lawyer," I say while bowing my neck with attitude.

"Yeah, you might want to do that. 'Cause I mean, you're going to jail for attempted murder and accessory to the fact, so yeah. You need a lawyer," he says sarcastically rolling his eyes.

"What? I have an alibi! I mean I at least know that much about the law. I had nothing to do with any of this! I already explained to you I was too scared to come forward! I didn't think he would do anything like this! Hell, y'all have a report of my gun is missing!"

"Yeah, THAT," Detective Prejean answers. "That is circumstantial evidence. Just saying. Girl, we know you are guilty and so do you. Just tell the truth and ease your mind!"

The fuck is he talking about? This is bullshit!

"Look, I want my lawyer and I want my lawyer now!" I demand.

"Okay, sure. Who is your lawyer?"

"I don't fucking know! But I'm supposed to get a call. I need a phone book and I want my call!" FUCK! Who is Janae's lawyer? This is some fucking bullshit! Like really! Shit! The fuck I'm supposed to do?

Janae has always been the person to handle shit like this! She was always the person to take charge and have all this shit in line. FUCK! Fuck this shit. I change my mind and my call goes to Peter...

"Hello?"

"Hello, Jazmynn?"

"Yes."

"Hey, sweetie. You okay?"

"Yeah, but I'm not sure how long this phone call lasts. I'm at the police station. I need a lawyer. I really don't know what all is going on, but I think they think I helped hurt Janae. They are trying to charge me with conspiracy!" Dong, dong, dong!

The call is cut off already. I hope he heard it all! Son of a bitch!

Peter's staff has been exceptional! I don't have to want for anything! But there's still one thing they can't give me. Janae. It's been three weeks and she's still in a coma. Here and there she responds with lifting a finger, but for the most part, it seems like she's completely out of it. I just want my friend back. I still haven't been able to go home yet, but I'm hoping they soon let me. I bought a few clothes, but I'm having to wear them over and over! The detectives have been here twice to re-question me and to question Peter, but there are no leads yet, and Devon has yet to be found. They finally let me go when Peter's lawyer submitted surveillance tapes of me at his house at the time the incident occurred.

I wonder where the hell Dev is. The neighbors say they haven't seen him come back to the house since the incident.

After a month, I have finally been granted the permission to re-enter my home and clean up. Peter sent some of his house cleaners with me to help. He is really being an exceptional guy. It's amazing how understanding and sweet he is. He hasn't changed one bit! Each day that goes by, I grow a love for him that he doesn't know about, and I don't think I want to tell him. Hell, I don't want things to end up like they ended up with Devon. I sigh. It's too soon to be thinking about a relationship with anyone anyway.

They finally were able to do surgery to remove the bullet and are now waiting on forensics to see what kind of gun the bullet came from. I'm an emotional wreck. Peter has been nothing but nice and is an awesome listener, but I can't help to wonder if he has anything to gain from being so good to me. Maybe he really does like me and this is really the man he is, then maybe he's another Devon… I know I probably need to quit comparing him to that piece of shit, but that piece of shit had me fooled really well. I wish I could talk to Janae. She would know exactly what to say at a time in my life like this. She always liked Peter. He really seems like the better man, but I guess only time will tell.

I've had to take a sick leave at work, which I will not be paid for, because I'm not actually sick, and because I haven't been working at the school long enough to acquire sick leave. This shit is driving me insane! I've missed graduation, I'm running out of money, and becoming sort of dependent on Peter. I'm beginning to hate myself. All of this is because of me. All of it. If I would've just left Devon alone, continued our friendship as it was, none of this would've ever happened! I cry almost every night and every time I think of everything that's going on.

Janae finally wakes from her coma and is well enough to speak to the detectives. She confirms what I had been trying to tell them the whole time. Most of it anyway. I found out that for sure Devon did this to her. I was hoping and praying it wasn't, and that he wouldn't do anything like this, but she confirmed my gut. The investigators put out a search warrant for him and it's been plastered all over the news. Still no Devon. It's like he's vanished.

"How are you feeling, Nae Nae?" I ask with tears in my eyes. I hate to see her like this. They've finally unplugged the majority of machines they had to her because she is finally breathing and eating on her own.

"Eh," she says, waving her right hand like "so-so." "I'm ready to go home though. I know that much."

"The nurse said it will still be a while before you can come home. You have a lot of therapy to do," I say sympathetically.

"Couldn't you just do the therapy? At home?" she asks meekly.

"I'm sorry, hun, no. I'm not qualified. But I can tell you what I can do! I will put an ad in the paper for a home care provider. They can help you during the day while I'm at work, and I can take care of you at night," I say, hoping she falls for it. I returned to work a couple days ago worried if I took any more days off I would be fired!

"Anything will beat staying in this motherfucker," she says, sounding annoyed.

I'm so glad that worked out. I was waiting for her to whine about how she doesn't like anyone in the house she doesn't know, and how I can YouTube how to take care of her. I left the hospital and went to the newspaper office, put the ad in, and it ran in the paper the very next day. I received more hits than I thought I would. My phone rang from 7:00 a.m. until 10:00 p.m. when I finally turned it completely off. I took off tomorrow from work to conduct interviews.

Sad to say I've seen twelve people in the last three hours, and none fit the description I put in the paper. I'm exhausted! One person doesn't change sheets, another isn't comfortable being away from home and wants to take her to his house for therapy. Another doesn't clean anything, because she's not planning to dirty anything. One needed her cell at all times (which rang at least four times interrupting the interview) and she needed to leave early Monday, Wednesday, and Friday because of her son's football practice. One girl said it would be her first job so she needed to be trained on what's expected for her to do. I have one more interview before lunch, and I hope so badly this one will be the one.

Susan. Redhead, thirty-year-old, certified nursing assistant with ten years of experience. She cooks, cleans, and the whole nine yards. Hired her on the spot.

Breaking news.

The body of an unidentified white male has been found this afternoon near the Mississippi River here in New Orleans, Louisiana, by some teens that were fishing. The New Orleans police department, Louisiana state police, and first response team responded to the call of the frantic teens in within minutes. Upon arrival, the officers located the body of the unidentified white male. The coroner stated the body had been deceased for at least a month looking at the stage of decomposition it was in. We will continue to update you on the story as any information comes in.

Knock, knock! I hear at the door. It's Detectives Lyneye and Prejean. What now?

Chapter 19

"Good morning, Ms. Barkley, may we come in?" asks Detective Lyneye.

"Yeah, sure," I say, swinging my hand, ushering them in.

"And for what do I owe this visit? Have y'all caught Devon?" I asked, eyes wide with excitement walking over turning down the TV.

"That's actually why we are here. Devon's body was found early this morning." Oh my goodness! Is that the body they were just talking about on the news? "We have reason to believe you are a suspect," answers Prejean with a devious grin.

"What?! Me? What in the hell are y'all talking about?" I say in total shock.

Janae comes, limping into the living room asking, "Hey, what's going on?"

"They say they found Devon's body this morning, and I'm a suspect!" I say to Janae.

"The fuck?" she says with a questioning look on her face. "Devon's body?! Devon's DEAD?" she says, cupping her mouth with her left hand in shock.

"Yes," answers Detective Lyneye. "And we are going to have to ask you to come in with us," she says apologetically, taking out her handcuffs.

"What the hell, man!" I yell. "Why? I don't know anything nor did I have anything to do with anything!" I scream as always. Lyneye grabs my left wrist and slaps the cuff on it, then grabs the other saying, "You have the right to remain silent. Anything you say can and will be held against you in a court of law. You have the right to an attorney. If you can't afford one, one will be provided for you at no cost from the court. Do you understand your rights?"

"Yes" I say in tears. "Janae, call Peter please!" I say as Janae stands staring in shock and they are taking me out of the door.

"The time of death has been narrowed down to the same night your friend Janae was beaten up. Were you angry and decided to take the law into your own hands? Here on this statement you have previously given, you accused him of raping you before all these events. Did you decide you had enough, couldn't take it anymore, and decided to kill him?" asks Prejean.

"No!" I never left the hospital! They know that! They have to know that! They questioned me for hours!

"The bullet that killed him is being analyzed as we speak, and when it comes back, it's from the gun you claim was stolen, you do know what that means right?" says Prejean.

"My gun was stolen, I was raped, and my friend was beaten up. So I guess all this is my fault? I'm the guilty one, okay," I say rhetorically.

"You can try to be funny if you want to, but I promise I will have the last laugh. Your gun, your bullet, and a dead boyfriend. Open and closed case. You killed him in a rage after he did what you said he did to you and no one believed you and threw his body in the Mississippi."

"Are you kidding me right now? How is that even possible? He's at least 200 pounds and I'm 130. Hell, I struggle to pick up a five-pound bag of potatoes!" I scream, completely dumbfounded. How could these accusations ever make sense?

The door flies open. A very handsome gentleman walks in dressed in a black suit and red polka-dotted tie with a briefcase. "My client will not be answering any more questions. Unless you have some hard evidence on her, I suggest you let her go."

"The murder weapon belongs to her," answers Prejean.

"So the forensics of the bullet is back? I doubt it. Try playing with somebody else. Jazmynn, let's go," he says to me.

"She is NOT to leave town!" I hear Prejean yell out as we leave.

I find out after being released the lawyer that had been handling all of this crazy shit was out of town and this one worked with him. Peter said they would both be representing me if any more foolishness became of all this crap.

Breaking news.

The unidentified body found on Wednesday, November 12, 2012, at approximately twelve in the afternoon near the Mississippi River has been identified as Devon Thomas, twenty-two, a New Orleans native. Thomas had a warrant out for his arrest for assault but was never apprehended. The Louisiana state Police ask if anyone has any information on this case to please call 1-800-496-TIPS.

Man. It's all over the news! I mean, all over. Now papers say I left Peter for Devon and killed Devon. I'm the prime suspect! I'm so lost and don't know what to do. Janae told me everything will blow over and be fine, but I just don't see it. All I can think about is the fact Devon is dead and I know me nor did Janae do it. I never told the police about Peter leaving the house, but now I'm kind of worried that Peter may have killed Devon and is going to let me take the wrap for it!

TAP, TAP! There goes another knock at the door. I stand to turn the TV down and walk to the door and peep through the peephole. It's Peter. Peter! The blood drains from my face I'm so scared. What if he really killed Devon? He said he would deal with him. What did he mean exactly? Shit!

"Well, are you going to invite me in?" he asks.

"Oh, yeah, sorry," I say, cautiously opening the door.

"How are you doing? Is everything okay?" he asks.

"Not good. Not good at all. I'm so lost and scared out of my mind!" I say, telling myself to ask him if he did it. Just ask him. You've known him long enough to tell if he's lying.

"Peter, did you..." I stop. Shit, this is harder than I thought. What if he goes off? What if he does tell me the truth? Shit, shit, shit!

"Did I what?" he asks, taking a seat at the bar on one of the stools.

"Did you kill Devon?" I sort of whispered. Janae is asleep; I feel the need to not talk too loud, but I'm terrified of what his response will be. I'm accusing him of murder. I'm not sure of how he will react, but I would probably be livid!

"Honestly, I would've if I would have found him that day. I was so angry that he had done that to you," he answers as if he's recalling that day. "I couldn't fucking find him, though. Somebody got to his ass before I could. But I tell you what, I'm glad he's dead. You should be too. A man like that doesn't deserve to live!" Peter says angrily, hitting the counter with his fist in a loud thud.

"I really don't know how to feel. He was a friend before all this, though. I just hate the not knowing what the fuck. Right now, everything is pointing to me and I don't even have the heart to kill a fly!" I said, bursting into tears. He comes over and wraps his arms around me kissing my temple. "It's okay, babe. I know, I know. It will all work itself out, just watch. You have some of the best lawyers in Louisiana on your team. They will do any and everything they can to help."

After a few minutes, the tears finally stop. I immediately feel tired. "Want to watch a movie?" I ask. Honestly, I already know I will be asleep within five minutes of the movie coming on, and he probably knows too, but he still says, "Sure."

We fix the pillows on my bed like a little fort. Each with a pillow on the outside of us, under our legs, and behind our backs, then turn off all the lights. As I go to turn the TV on with the remote, I notice a red beam of light coming from one of my picture frames on my dresser. Peter asks, "What the hell is that?" pointing at it.

I flip on my lamp and begin to get up to go toward it. "Hell, I don't know!" I say confused. I look to the area I saw the light beaming from and there's a small circular thing with a wire attached to the picture frame. I unhook the back of the frame and the object falls out. I pick it up and it looks like some sort of tiny camera. It's no bigger than my index finger! I turn it over and there's a tiny on and off switch. I switch it to on. Click! That sounds soooo familiar. Click! I turn it back off. I then walk over to Peter to show it to him.

"It's a camera," he says. "I've seen these before. You can set them to record, take pictures, and stream over the internet directly to your computer. Almost like a nanny cam. Where does it come from? Do you think someone has been recording you? If the police put this here, it's definitely a violation of privacy! I should call your lawyer," he says, standing to his feet, digging in his pocket for his cell phone.

"Shit, I don't know! But you know what?" I say, sitting on the edge of the bed. "This is maybe a little too much information, but one day, me and Devon were about to have sex and I heard that same click. He had my face covered with a pillow, so I couldn't see exactly what he was doing! Do you think that bastard was recording me?" I say as though I'm asking myself.

"Well, let's find out, where's your laptop? Let's see what's on here," Peter says. I grab my laptop, but then we both look at each other realize we don't have a plug to connect the camera to the computer. We come to the conclusion silently but completely in sync.

"Let's go buy one," Peter says. "This may be just what the police need to see what a sick motherfucker he really was if it is, in fact, him who planted it!"

We finally get back from the store after going in about ten of them before finding the right cord and connect the camera to the computer and oh my God! There are pictures on top of pictures of me and several videos. The pictures show me sleeping, reading magazines, on the phone, dressing, and masturbating! I gasp and cover my mouth with my left hand. How embarrassing! I slam close the laptop.

"What you go do that for? We need to look at all of them! He might be in one to prove how sick he is," says Peter.

"Oh, hell no! I'm not letting the police see this! It's too embarrassing! I'm naked, half naked, and you know... I sort of kind of play with my sex toy from time to time. See I was single for a good while, and..." Holding my index finger up, "But anyway, this is in the privacy of my own room! This is so embarrassing!" I say beginning to tear up.

Peter leans over and embraces me once again. "Jazmynn, I don't care about any of that! That's personal, and yes, maybe a little embarrassing, but it's your business! I cannot judge you!" He picks my head up by my chin and kisses me on the lips. Soft, sweet, enticing. I want more. I need more. I lean in closer and begin to kiss him. Let me show him exactly how bad I want it.

I nip at his bottom lip, encouraging the tiger to come out of him. This time, he doesn't stop me. I spin us around, making his back face the bed and push him onto it. I lean over and grab my computer sitting it on the floor and sliding it under the bed laying the tiny camera on top of it. He's lying face up smiling the sexiest smile a man can smile in a moment like this. He pulls off his shirt, and I follow suit, exposing my gorgeous breasts to him once more. The first time he saw them, the gentleman in him made him stop the thoughts he had because he knew I was taken. Now, I'm fair game! I unfasten his belt, then the button on his pants. I notice he has already kicked off his shoes. I decide to do sort of a strip tease for him to remove the last of my clothes. I remove his pants first so now he is just lying on the bed in his boxers. I stand to my feet with my back to him and pull my pants down. Slowly. Very slowly. When I finally made them reach my ankles and peeked back at Peter to make sure he was enjoying his view, he definitely was, if you know what I mean. (Hard as a fucking rock!)

I decide to leave on my matching panties and bra for a little while. I climb back into bed and straddle him. I find the hole in his boxers and whip his big ass pleasure rod. Lawd. Devon thought he was laying pipe. Devon didn't have shit on Peter. This motherfucker here hung son! Just looking at his pleasure rod makes me want to release. But I know I can't do that just yet. I have a little work to do. I begin kissing his stomach up to his chest, then to the right side of his neck then back down. I finally lean in and caress his mouth with mine. Lightly at first. His lips are so soft and smooth. He grabs the back of my neck and returns with something stronger. His mouth tastes of mint. He gazes deeply into my eyes and I see another part of him. He pulls back and smiles. He seems to be enjoying the whole charade. As I bite my bottom lip, I go ahead and take his boxers off. I grab his pleasure rod with my left hand and slowly stroke it up and down. Just enough to let him know how I want it. Gently and slow.

I sit completely up placing my hands on his muscular chest and he grabs both ass cheeks and picks me up and down. Shit. I guess he's telling me how he plans on doing me! We begin to kiss once more. This time, it felt different. A good different. It felt like love. It gave me the feeling that this is what I want for the rest of my life. It made me feel this was good for me and he was who I needed.

He then places his right hand on my left ass check while his left-hand grabs his pleasure rod waiting for me bounce on it. I take his right hand from my ass and put it on my left breast, then I take his left off his pipe and put on my right breast and he goes to work massaging and squeezing away never losing eye contact. I lean forward a little and slide my panties to the side with my left hand and use my right to insert his pipe into my happy place. I have to do a little wiggling to get it in right, but I finally do. Once he was fully inserted, I release. I tried not to but I guess all the built-up stress and fuckstration, I just don't know! I start rocking on his pleasure rod hard. He sits up and begins to lick my right nipple, and I grab his head with my right hand keeping a steady motion. Back and forth. It feels like he goes deeper into me with every stroke. Mmm. This shit feels so fucking good! I'm guessing it feels even better to him because he has now grabbed my ass with both hands and is answering to each thrust with a light smack on each ass cheek. It makes me even hornier. I release again. "Yes, baby, get you," Peter whispers in my ear.

"Yes! Yes! UH! Mhmm. Like that! Just like that!" I yell. With a quick swoop, he flips me on my back, never exiting his wonderful pipeline of a pipe. He slows down a little. Winding, then grinding. He pulls out, pulls my panties off, throwing them on the floor and thrusts that pipe back in. Mhmm. I like that! Completely in, then pulls out. I feel like I'm about to release AGAIN! Damn! I've never gone this many times at once with Dev! Hell, I damn near faked all of them with him! He pulls completely out and starts to lick my sweet spot. I never knew a tongue could move so fast! I release again and again! I had to tell him to stop. My lady garden became soooo sensitive. One touch and I tremble! I needed a breather. Just knowing his face was down there made me want to release again. I was beyond sensitive down there. I could barely move my legs without the vibration in my lady garden wanting to release again. I sit up, and he is laying on his side with his left hand holding up his head.

"How much longer?" he asks hungrily with a smile brighter than the sun.

"Boy! A year! Shit, I've never had this much pleasure. Like ever!" I say, overwhelmed. My vagina is still thumping.

He sits up and starts looking around the floor for something. Is he looking for his boxers and pants? "What are you doing?" I ask, alarmed. I was only kidding about the year thing. Please don't leave! I scream to myself. "I was just kidding."

"Girl, I know," he says with a smirk on his face easing out of bed finally finding and slipping on his boxers. "I have to take a piss, bathroom?" he replies.

"Oh! First door to the left," I say relieved. I thought he was leaving, and I most definitely don't want this moment to end. He throws on my robe and eases out of the room. I lay back on the bed in a supine position. Ahh! I sigh loudly. Damn, he did that! I never thought sex would or could be so magical. I never really had this with Dev. It was all about him. His pleasure. Mind you, all the time wasn't the worst, but I can definitely count the times it was enjoyable!

He reenters the room and thinking about all the fun we have just had, I've gotten a little sleepy. There's no way I can do that to him, though, right? No. I couldn't. I've just had the most amazing sex of my life! I'm weak and tired, but it's his pleasurable moment now. I sit back up and using my index finger I motion for him to come to me. He takes off my robe and lays on side of me as he was before with his hand holding his head up. I lean in to kiss him. He gently kisses back, eventually removing his hand from his head and placing me on my back. He grabs at my right breast and begins sucking and licking my neck slowly moving down to my left breast. His right hand slides down my body to my left thigh picking it up from underneath. He gently runs his fingers up and down my inner thighs, passing a finger through my lady garden. He begins rubbing my sweet spot slowly in a circular motion, almost entering my lady garden, but just enough to spread the water around my lady garden. He sticks his middle finger in my lady garden with his thumb, never leaving my sweet spot.

Mmm. I moan in his mouth as it has made its way back up to me. "Turn on your side," he whispers.

My side? The hell? I wonder, but do as I'm told. "No, baby, your other side. With your back to me." He giggles. I reluctantly do. This starts to remind me of Dev in the shower. That hurts. "I don't like this," I say.

"Oh, but you will," he says confidently. He lifts my right leg and gently slides his pipe into my lady garden. He pumps a couple times, hitting a spot I never knew was there. "Oooohh!" I gasp in pleasure. He slides his left arm under my neck, grabbing at my left breast and gets closer to me. It's like we're spooning, but a little uncomfortable. His arm under my neck is giving me a Charlie horse. He must've noticed that I was uncomfortable because before I knew it, I was lying face-down, and he was on top of me from behind. My legs are slightly open but completely straight. I turn my head to the side to breathe reaching my hands above my head placing them flat on the headboard of the bed. My lady garden feels every inch of his wonderful pleasure rod. In and out, he humps smacking my ass with each stroke. He thrusts inside with such precision. Hitting that spot every single time. I can't move much, but each thrust he takes I tilt my ass up to him to ensure he goes deeper. He may not even be going deeper, but I sure feel like it! He lays on my back and begins kissing my neck with both arms at each side of me holding himself up by his elbows, and whispers, "Damn, girl. This feels good!"

"It's yours, Daddy, take it. It's just for you!" I scream in ecstasy and so does he, going in with hard thrusts.

"Ugh! Mhmm. Shit, girl. Mmm." His thrusts slow and he's starting to shake at the end of each stroke, as he wraps his right arm around my neck and is tugging away at my left ass cheek with his left. He loosens his grip and stops moving with his pipe buried away in my lady garden and his head face down in the pillow on side of my head. It can stay there for all I care. That's where it now belongs, I say to myself.

He turns me on my right side as he turns. Moving strands of hair out of his way to kiss my neck and ear. "I don't want to run you off," he whispers. "I hope you never leave because I think I'm in love with you," he says.

I don't know what to say. I mean, I like Peter, and all this was nice and all, but love? I think I may love him back—hell, I know I do, but the last person I told I loved them fucked over me. He is now dead and still fucking over me. Peter has stood by my side through all the bullshit though. I have to say that is a plus.

I can't tell him I love him too. I just can't. It's just too soon… "I'm not going anywhere," I finally answer and we fall asleep.

Chapter 20

The Arraignment

We awake to a knock at the bedroom door saying it's the police. How the fuck they even got in the house? The police? A-fucking-gain? What the fuck man?! Peter jumps up looking puzzled and grabs my robe for me to put on throwing it to me. Once I've covered my body, he opens the door.

"Jazmynn Olivia Barkley, you are under arrest for the murder of Devon Edward Thomas. You have the right to remain silent. Anything you say can and will be held against you in the court of law. You have the right to an attorney. If you cannot afford an attorney, one will be provided for you. Do you understand your rights?" I'm asked while they are putting the cuffs on me.

"Would y'all at least let her get dressed first?" asks Peter, standing in just his boxers with concern written all over his face.

"Nope. We have orders to take her in as soon as possible," answers one of the Louisiana state police officers dryly. "She will have an attorney. What is she even being charged with?" asks Peter with a questioning look on his face.

"Sir, attempted murder for a Ms. Janae Carter, and first-degree murder of Mr. Devon Thomas," answered the snobby officer and out the door, we went. "I will call the lawyer!" Peter bellows out to me in a high-pitched voice like he is getting ready to burst into tears.

Once we arrive at the precinct, I am ordered to take off my robe and put on a filthy-looking orange jumpsuit. After completing the task, I was brought into an interrogation room where more bullshit began.

"We received the records from Mr. Thomas's phone. The text messages are what we are the most concerned with and are part of the reason you are being charged with murder. We have one that states, and I quote, 'Leave me the fuck alone. It's none of your business where I am. You will never find me and if you ever try to do that shit to me again. I WILL KILL YOU, you sick bastard!' This message comes from you approximately two hours before Devon was murdered. Can you explain this?" asks Detective Lyneye.

I'm sitting here, freezing my ass off in only that orange jumpsuit. No shoes no under clothes, no nothing. "Yes, I can," I say. "He raped me and sent messages of how he was sorry and asking me where I was and all kind of bullshit. I was livid and hurt that he would do that to me."

"So you killed him in revenge?" asks Lyneye, raising her left eyebrow in shock.

"No. I was still at Peter's house. I was there the entire time the shit happened to Janae and I guess during the time of the murder."

"You guess?" she asks as if she's catching me in some sort of lie. I guess she's not on my side anymore. Either that or she's trying to play bad good cop bad cop. "No, I'm sure," I answer with a complete attitude. "Can y'all give me a blanket? I'm freezing!"

"Hmm! The temperature in here is fine. I'm comfortable, but, sweetheart," she says leaning over the table, "that's the least of your worries right now. Where you are going, you will need this air conditioning!" says Lyneye pouring a glass of water. The bitch is fully dressed. Of course, the temperature is comfortable for her! Whatever happened to that lady I spoke to before? She has completely changed to this cold-hearted bitch cop!

"Can you explain why one of the missing bullets from your gun was found to be one of the bullets that killed Devon? How about the fact it is also the gun that shot Janae? Or is your gun still stolen like you said the last time?" she asks the last question sarcastically.

"No, I cannot," I answer simply. It really doesn't matter what I say to her, everything points to me and that's what she is going with. All I can do is not allow her or anyone else to break me down and make me confess to something I had no dealings with.

"Okay, suit yourself!" Lyneye says, standing and heading to the door. "You may want to take a plea deal 'cause, girl, with murder, you are going away for a long ass time!" she snickers, leaving out of the interrogation room.

An officer comes to get me and brings me to a holding cell. He throws some dirty, dingy white jumpsuit that has LCIW stamped on the front of it with a T-shirt and tells me to give him my orange one. "May I have a little privacy?" I ask quietly. "No can do," he says, smiling from ear to ear. "Dere ain't no privacy at St. Gabriel, girl. You gone have to learn to dress, bathe, and shit wit people lookin at chew," he snickers, twirling a piece of straw in his mouth, and he doesn't turn around!

I turn my back to him and pull the orange jumpsuit down and put on my shirt. I then turned back to face him bending over toward the wall while quickly stepping out of the orange suit into the white. I finally finish and toss the jumpsuit at him while walking over to sit on the bench. I begin to cry. What the hell has happened to my life? I probably no longer have a job, a man, hell, or a best friend. Would Janae disown me? No. She wouldn't. She knows me better than this. This is not me! I am not a murderer!

After about two hours I was transported to St. Gabriel, Louisiana also known as the Louisiana Correctional Institute for Women. As I walk in with several other women handcuffed, women are screaming, "Fresh meat! Fresh meat! I call the sexy chocolate one." Another says, "I call the Mexican!" And so forth as if we are on auction. I am terrified. Some of these women look like men! It's too much that it's beyond scary. I make it to a cell and the guard tells me to enter and closes the gate. He then tells me to put my hands in a little rectangular hole to take off my handcuffs. I look around the cell. There are a couple pictures on the walls of a little girl and a little boy and different pictures of drawings of dragons. That shit freaks me out even more! I take one peek out of the cell and begin crying. This is not the life for me! I don't deserve this! I turn to the bottom bunk and decide to sit. After a few minutes, I decide to lie down and fell fast asleep.

I attend court the next morning in shackles. Fucking shackles! Both of my hands are handcuffed together in the front of me and my feet are handcuffed together with chains. The guards march me and a couple other inmates down a hall to the left and onto a bus. We ride roughly fifteen minutes before stopping in front of the courthouse. We exit one by one with one guard pointing a shotgun at each one of our heads. This is beyond bullshit because I am not a criminal!

I begin to think to myself about the fact that, it's funny how a person is supposed to be innocent until proven guilty, but I've been having to sit my ass in a jail cell because of a charge I haven't been convicted of yet! But I'm innocent until proven guilty, yeah, okay. More like guilty until proven innocent!

We (the inmates) walk in a single file line entering a side door of the courthouse, which brings us down a hall. Three lefts and one right later we end up in a courtroom. The guards point to us and tell us to take a seat, which is in the jury box. We all sit looking around at the empty courtroom. It's quiet until one of the inmates start talking to someone on side of her, they both giggle uncontrollably, and the guards say to shut up. The district attorney, Authur Bushwell, walks in with authority. Black suit and blue tie. He sounds like he has on high heeled shoes too, ol punk ass. He glances at us in the jury box and quickly turns his head doing his very best to not make eye contact. Three more lawyers walk in, two sit with the district attorney, and one at the defense attorney's desk. The minute clerk, law clerk, and court reporter enter, and so does several spectators. Some sit in front of the partition and the others sit behind the partition closer to where the judge sits. Suddenly people start piling in, so I'm guessing court is getting ready to start. The door continues to open and close open and close. Then I see Peter, the two lawyers, and Janae. Tears build up in my eyes. I hope the money Peter is paying these lawyers works in the best interest of me. They wave and smile at me sympathetically and I begin to cry. I feel so helpless and worthless.

The bailiff comes out some little door by the judge's bench and says, "All rise! Thirty-third Criminal District Court is now in session. The honorable Judge, Charlotte E. Francis, presiding."

"Good morning, ladies and gentlemen. Please turn your attention to the left corner where our American flag is. Please place your right hand over your heart and recite with me the pledge of allegiance," says Judge Francis.

We all do what she says in unison.

"You may now be seated," says the bailiff.

Judge Francis sits. Then she opens a laptop, pulls out a notepad while looking around, finally finding a pen to her far left. She says something about good morning to you too and thanks to you officer then begins talking to someone on the laptop. As quiet as it is in here, it's hard to hear the conversation. The district attorney and the other lawyers that are with him are huddled and whispering. I hear something about the person being charged with domestic violence, violence on a police officer, and something about a fistic encounter. The person on the other end replies yes to Judge Francis's question if they understood. Then Judge Francis says the bond is set at four-thousand dollars for the first charge, fifty-five hundred for the second, and one thousand for the third. She thanks the officer once again and closes the laptop turning her attention to the lawyers.

"Calling the case of the people of Louisiana vs. Sarah Blue. Are both sides ready?" asks Judge Francis.

The district attorney stands and says, "Yes, your honor, if it pleases the court, my name is Authur Bushwell and I appear for the prosecution."

The defense lawyer then stands. "Yes, your honor, if it pleases the court, my name is James Roggerson and I appear for the defense."

Judge Francis says, "Thank you, counsel. Please read the charges to the accused."

One of the guards stands as one of the women with us and walks her to the dock.

"We are here today with case number 12-1-00058-5," says one of the ladies sitting by the judge. Sarah Blue, you have been charged under section 19AA of the Criminal Law Consolidation Act 2012 of the unlawful stalking of Robert Petterson between August 2011 to February 2012. How do you plead?"

"I am certainly NOT guilty!" screams Sarah Blue in a high-pitched voice.

The officer goes back up to her and grabs her arm leading her to sit back down with us.

"This is BULLSHIT!" she squeals before Judge Francis tells her, "One more outburst and you will be found in contempt. This is not how things are handled in my courtroom missy, put a lid on it!"

"Ahm. Would the prosecution please read the names of witnesses it will be called upon for evidence? Prospective jurors, please listen carefully to the names called and let me know if you have any association with them."

District Attorney Bushwell stands and states, "The prosecution will be calling the victim Robert Petterson, his mother Georgia Petterson, the victim's friend Patricia McArthy, and Karista Blue the defendant's sister."

"Does any of the prospective jurors know any of the witnesses? Please stand," asks Judge Francis, looking across the courtroom.

Two people stand almost in unison. A man and a woman on the right side of the courtroom. Judge Francis motions for them to come up to the bench. The woman shuffles to the bench wearing a pink and white floral two-pieced suit with baby doll heels to match. The gentleman without losing stride follows suit wearing only a T-shirt and a pair of jeans with tennis shoes. The woman whispered something to the judge with the man doing the same. But Judge Francis only nods back. Both lawyers have now approached the bench, and each is taking turns talking. Either one shakes his head no, or the other waves his left-hand motioning no. People begin to whisper a little around the courtroom. I find myself looking back in the area Peter and Janae were sitting. Janae is still there but Peter and the lawyers are gone. Janae looks at her watch it seems like every five minutes like she does when she has somewhere better to be. Maybe she does. Or maybe she just misses me as much as I miss her, and this process is taking too damn long! I've only been locked up for a day, but I promise when I get out; I will get me a dog. It won't stay in a cage, it will eat when it wants, and I promise to wash its bedding! That dog won't know it's a dog. It's going to think it's a person and be treated like a person should! I never knew people in jail lived like wild animals. I understand some should be there for different crimes they've committed, but damn. What about the ones like me that haven't done anything but pay taxes, work, and are innocent?!

Sarah Blue grabs the attention of one of the officers and mouthed for him to come to see her, please. He leans over to listen and immediately shakes his head no. She mouthed, please. He says no once again beginning to walk away and she reaches out and grabs his elbow. He stops, looks at her, and said, "WAIT!" Shrugging his arm out of her grab. Probably a little louder than he initially meant to because he sort of jumped and then looked around. He caught eye contact with another guard and mouthed "bathroom" sarcastically with an annoyed look on his face.

The man and woman walk away from the bench and out the door of the courtroom, and both lawyers walk back to their posts. The guard who talked to Sarah walked over to the defense attorney and whispered something in his ear. He looks at the guard for a second, nods, and raises his right hand beginning to stand to place his left on the table in front of him.

"Your honor, if I may?" he asks, waiting patiently for an answer. Judge Francis who is looking down at some papers in front of her, glances up. "Proceed."

"Your honor, the defense motions for a quick recess." Judge Francis looked at him sideways, took a deep breath, while shaking her head and saying, "Motion granted. Court will reconvene today at 11:00 a.m."

People begin to mummer in frustration. They look at the defense lawyer with daggers in their eyes. What's all that about? Let's get this shit over with. I'm starving, man! The guard walks over to the jury stand and asks does anyone else need the restroom. One of the other girls reply yes, and they tell her to come with them. They walk Sarah Blue and the other girl out of the door we first entered. A couple spectators get up and walk out and I see a few people who were sitting in the audience get up with boxes of cigarettes and lighters as if they are going take a smoke break, everyone else remains seated and the low mummers turn into louder conversations. Janae catches my eye and gives me a thumb-up sign while winking. She looks scared shitless but knows she must maintain her strength for me and my sanity. If she breaks, I break. All I can do is wonder what time it is. Why isn't everyone leaving?

I see Robert Peterson and his mother whispering to each other. He says something to her and she nods her head in agreement. The door opens from where we entered, and he starts fidgeting. Sarah Blue must be one bad bitch. He looks toward the door and breathes a sigh of relief when he realizes it's just one of the spectators returning. He returns to his conversation with his mother. Karista Blue, Sarah Blue's sister, and Patricia McCarthy sit opposite of Robert and his mother. They exchange glances but never speak. Karista looks as though she wants to burst into tears, while Patricia looks like she's ready to kill. She keeps her face in a pouted position like she's annoyed and would rather be somewhere else. I notice Peter sticking his head in the door and calling Janae's name. She turns around, nods, and gets up turning to walk out. She looks back at me holding her index finger up and mouths "Be right back." Then exits the courtroom. Every time someone enters or exits, I try to see if I can see them outside the door but see nothing but a wall and hallway. My anxiety is at a new high. I'm worried about what this day will bring and pray it's all going to be over soon!

It feels like an eternity before I see Janae, Peter, and the two lawyers re-enter. As they do, spectators and all others who left out begin to re-enter as well. The two lawyers walk up to the defense lawyer and say something to him. He puts his left hand out saying something while shaking his head no. My handsome lawyer says above a whisper, "We want to consult with our client now! It will only take a minute, shit she's right there!" he says, impatiently pointing in my direction. In the corner of my eye, I notice the side door we entered in opens and Sarah Blue and the other girl is returning with the guards. Sarah yanks her arm out of the guard's grasp and says, "You're hurting me!" in her high-pitched voice and stops walking. My lawyers walk over to the jury box and the handsome one motions with his finger for me to come to see. I glance back at the two guards with Sarah and the other girl and they aren't even paying me any attention. I start walking over to the lawyers and Sarah begins cursing the guard while pulling out of his grasp again this time stumbling toward where I am getting ready to go down the steps. Before I know it, the other girl goes for the guard's gun that is holding her. The guard standing with Sarah turns to help throw the girl on the ground leaving Sarah unattended. Sarah in one quick swoop grabs his nine-millimeter gun and shoots both guards turning pointing the gun at the audience pulling the trigger at Karista, Patricia, Robert, and his mother, hitting all four targets with one bullet a piece!

Right as I'm getting ready to fall to the ground, I notice the judge entering saying, "WHAT THE HELL?" And Sarah turns the gun her way, pulling the trigger hitting the judge in the neck, making her collapse on her podium. The blood drains from my face as I hear Janae scream my name. I go down hard. I can't hear anything out of my left ear but muffles and a high-pitched note. I hear something like, "What are you doing? This isn't part of the plan!" Then I hear one more shot ring out before Sarah Blue falls on top of me. People are screaming and running. I can hear Janae screaming, "Jazmynn! Jazmynn!"

The weight of Sarah is lifted off me and I turn my head to see one of my lawyers checking for her pulse. The other lawyer grabs me and picks me up bringing me down the steps and laying me on the floor. He says, "Can you hear me? Jazmynn, can you hear me?"

I nod my head yes and look behind him to see Peter. He steps from behind and kneels asking me if I'm all right. I nod my head once more as he leans over and kisses my forehead before the handsome lawyer tells him he has to go back to his seat.

Police and swat swarm the courtroom and I faint.

Chapter 21

I've been cellmates with this girl named Narasha for two damn months. Either my lawyer asks for some kind of stupid-ass extension, or the district attorney files some new motion. The district attorney wants to continue the case with another judge, but my lawyers don't think it's in my best interest. The judge was just recently let out of the intensive care unit and will have to have therapy. This is bad. Really bad.

Anyway, I've been in this bitch entirely too long! I'm beyond ready to go home to sleep in my own soft bed, eat real food, and shit in peace. Without an audience, without being embarrassed to change a tampon, and to be able to have personal space again.

Narasha and I have become pretty cool, but she will never amount to Janae. I talk to Janae and Peter twice a day for ten minutes apiece. Peter has kept me with money and minute cards, so I can always keep in touch with the both of them. Peter told me he took the pictures and videos we found to the lawyers he hired for me and they noticed a guy on several of the videos that they weren't positive was Dev. They are having some high-tech guys look at the film and try to blow up the face of the guy seen. They said he favors Dev's persona but his mannerism is different. They are beginning to think Dev may have multiple personalities. They said some of the videos he seems to be cool, calm, and collected, but in others, he's edgy, irritable, and always looking over his shoulders.

My arraignment has finally been reset and I'm an emotional wreck. I'm sooooo nervous, but Narasha keeps telling me it will be fine, I may just have to do about five to seven years, but I can't settle for doing time for a crime I have not committed! I'm so ready to get this over with, but I feel all evidence point to me, and I may spend the rest of my life in this hell hole. I really hope these lawyers know what they are doing and get me the hell out of here. I'd rather die than spend one more hour in here.

It's our free hour to go outside or watch TV in the common area. Today I just don't feel like looking at the sun I won't be able to see freely again so I tell Narasha I'm staying in to watch television. She decides to stay with me for support, so we grab a seat near the TV, which was playing I love Lucy and the guard abruptly changes the station to the news. "Awe, man, bro!" I yelled, throwing my hands in the air. Then I hear…

> In the news today. Scandalous Jazmynn is what she's being called nowadays. Jazmynn Olivia Barkley, twenty-six years old, BFM, born May 24, 1986, will be arraigned for the murder of her estranged boyfriend in the morning beginning at eight o'clock. We aren't sure if you remember the story, but the suspect Ms. Barkley was the highlight of some magazines and newspapers almost a year ago for being the mystery woman in well-known entrepreneur Peter Williamson's life. She was the guidance counselor at Dillard University who is being accused of murdering her boyfriend, Devon Thomas, twenty-two years old, BM, born March 15, 1990, out of a jealous rage. Devon Thomas's body was found November 12, 2012, by native teens that were fishing along the east of the Mississippi River. Detectives later learned the identity of the person allegedly responsible for the death of Devon Thomas after forensics from a bullet of a gun owned by Jazmynn Barkley

returned. Ms. Barkley was taken into custody without incident. Ms. Barkley was booked into the Louisiana Correctional Institute for women in St. Gabriel, Louisiana, for first-degree murder of Devon Thomas, and attempted murder of a Janae Carter, which she allegedly shot with the same gun at a separate time. No bond was set.

"Whoa! Hold up, girl! That's who you going to trial for murdering? Shit, I would've thought somebody would have murdered Evon's evil ass first," says Narasha in total shock.

"Shhh! Let me listen," I shush her, interested in what's being said about me. They have it all wrong and when I get out, I will sue their asses for slander! I'm so mad I can spit fire!

The news lady continues with, "Devon's twin brother Evon featured here (on screen) is at a loss for words. He allowed an interview which we have parts of and will now show."

Evon?! What the fuck? That's Devon. What the fuck is he doing? What is he up to? I scream inwardly.

"Hi, Mr. Thomas, my name is Emily Fontenot with WWL-TV channel 4 news. I'm here to interview you on the death of your brother Devon Thomas. Which his body was found November 12 of last year along the Mississippi River. Can you tell us what you know?" asks the reporter.

"Yeah, man, she was sleeping with the both of us."

"And saying she, you mean Jazmynn Barkley?" asks the reporter.

"Yeah, and when I confronted her about it, she denied it. I can't believe she killed my brother, man, trying to kill me! I'm so torn! It's like a piece of me is gone." He fake sniffles. "They both were my world, but my brother was a piece of me. We shared the same blood type and everything."

I can't take any more of this! What the hell is going on?! Shut the front door! Devon had a fucking twin? A TWIN? I stand to my feet and run to the payphone to call Janae.

"Hello?"

"Nae Nae, it's me. You watching the news?"

"Girl, yes, and I'm already on it. Did you know Dev had a twin?" she asks.

"Girl, hell no! But that may explain the different moods and change of attitude..." I say, beginning to think of past scenarios.

"That motherfucker!" shouts Janae, throwing something against the wall. "Well, I'll be damned. You gonna have to call me later. I need to find this twin and get to the bottom of this shit before court in the morning. I will be there and so will Peter. Keep your head up, I love you, you will be out soon. Bet that!" Janae says, hanging up the phone.

I call Peter. No answer. Shit!

So all this time I think I'm tripping and Devon is acting strange and those times it really wasn't Devon? It couldn't have been. It was like day and night. I noticed the difference and still was clueless. No stupid. Wow. This shit isn't making sense to me. How could Devon allow Evon to deceit me like this? Was he in on it? Like, some kind of a sick joke between the two? Or did he even know? Hell, how could I have not known? I found it weird he would leave to go to the park from time to time and fifteen minutes later be back wanting to have sex again, but hell, I just figured he was a horny guy who couldn't get enough! Then again, I found it unearthly for him to be soft and sensual, but an hour later roaring like a tiger. How could I have not known? Am I really that stupid?! Like how? Was it he who broke into my house and tied me to the chair and stole my gun? I'm completely lost. I don't know what to think. I'm so angry, frustrated, and confused. So was it Evon who raped me and beat Janae barricading her in her room leaving her to die? Why? Did he set that up not expecting me to come when I did and find her? Then when I did, and he saw I was with Peter, did he think it was Dev's fault and kill him? Did he even see me come home? Did he leave Janae for dead? All these questions run through my head and I don't have an answer for not even one! I begin baring my teeth feeling flushed. My muscles tense and my mouth become dry. I will never forgive Dev. I wish he was still alive, so I could kill him myself! The betrayal and hurt I feel is unexplainable. I go back to my cell and lay on my cot, plotting some kind of revenge on this brother Evon.

Meanwhile, Janae has found Evon's hiding spot. She called a few of her contacts down at the police station and was able to get his address. He was living in a hotel room across town. She took a cab there and knocked on the door. Evon opens the door and immediately attempts to shut it but Janae wedges her foot in.

"You are going to open this door, and you are going to let me in," she demands in a stern voice.

He reluctantly does, and she enters. When she walks in, he slams the door behind her making her jump. As she looks around the room, she notices pictures of me all over the walls and floors. Sleeping, naked, on the runway, with Dev (or him), in Las Vegas, standing in the window at work. She gasps! "Have you been stalking Jazmynn?!" She turns and asks him, noticing panties and bras thrown out across the bed.

"Well, I wouldn't quite call it stalking being she's been with me willingly and sleeping with me and all," Evon says with a sly grin. "I mean, she even told me she loved me."

"You are a sick bastard! You know Jazmynn knew nothing about you! You were raping her! Damn, you killed Dev, didn't you?" she asks, squinting her eyes madder than a shot wild hog. Steam flies out of her ears like on the cartoons.

"Ahahah! Now is that the way you treat your roommate?" Evon says, shaking his finger at Janae saying "no," smiling a devious grin.

"Here!" he pulls a chair out. "I'm glad you came, have a seat," he says calmly.

She walks briskly up to him. "I don't want to fucking sit, I want fucking answers!" She yells, spitting into his face. He grabs her, and physically sits her down, and says, "Girl, shut the fuck up and sit your ass down! Let me explain this shit to you if you don't already know. I run this, been running this. Soon as they send that scandalous friend of yours back to jail from her arraignment until her trial, you will be free to go. You go to the police, and you will end up like my long-lost brother, SWIMMING WITH THE GATORS!" He begins laughing, turning on the television. "Do we have an understanding?" he asks, seemingly not to truly care what her answer is.

"So you did kill him?" asks Janae, never answering his question, but now terrified not knowing what his next move is.

"Why would I want to kill my brother?" Evon asks as if he's in total shock putting his hand over his heart then slapping it down on his knee laughing. "I loved my brother. He was a little soft at times, but I still loved him," he says, placing his right hand over his heart once again. "I loved Jazmynn more, though. I don't know why the bitch had to always choose my brother over me!" he says, angrily removing his hand from his heart and balling it into a fist.

"All I did for her, all I've invested," he says, walking over to sit in a chair at the desk near the window.

"Well, guess what? You're right! You are not who she wanted, and Devon was the best man! So now what? And invested? The fuck you invested in her? Heartache? Pain? Grief?" says Janae, whirling her hands around angrily. "You need to get yourself checked into some kind of facility or turn yourself in. You won't get away with this Evon." Janae sneers. Evon opens a drawer on the desk and pulls out some gray tape, jumps up, and attempts to tape Janae's mouth but she begins screaming for help while digging in her bag for her mace. He grabbed her by the neck with one hand, saying, "See, bitch, that's your problem. You don't know when to shut the fuck up. There are times to speak and times to listen. You try to act all hard and like you know everything, but you are dumb as fuck. You so dumb, you about to make me kill you because of your loud ass fucking mouth! Now, I'm about to put this tape on those black ass lips you got, and we are going to sit here and watch a little television in silence. I know you don't know what that is, but you will learn soon if I hear as much as a sneeze out of your ass." He lets go of her throat and she screams again from the top of her lungs. That was it. He had had enough. He did all he knew to do. Struck her right across her left temple, knocking her out putting her to sleep. He hit her so hard she flew out of her chair, almost sliding under the foot of the bed. He dragged her to the opening of the room and began taping her hands together following with her ankles and put a piece over her mouth all the way around her head. He picked her up and slung her on the bed snickering, "I told you that you couldn't shut the fuck up. Nightie, night, bitch!"

Chapter 22

My Fate in Two Words

It's 7:00 a.m. I tried to call Janae and Peter two more times before lights out but got neither one of them. I barely slept, thinking of what this day could possibly bring. In one sense I'm hoping the court attempts to show leniency, but in another, I hope they somehow realize what a piece of shit Dev's brother Evon actually is. All that fake crying and shit he did during that interview. Nobody needs to feel sorry for his ass. At least not just yet.

Anyway, I hope they see that I have no prior record and just dismiss all charges against me. If my lawyers are as good as Peter says, they should be able to at least get me out on bond. I hope and pray. That's really about all I can do. My gun was found with only my prints on it. I don't know how the fuck that was even possible, but that's what I was told. The bullet that was pulled out of Janae's chest and the bullet that killed Dev both matched. I don't know what I'm going to do, but I do know I'm scared as shit. There's no way I will last in jail another day. A guard comes to get me out of my cell and Narasha hugs me telling me everything is going to be okay. She's praying for me, and to keep my head positive.

I take a deep breath in, exhaling slowly. That's easier said than done.

It was the same routine as the last. We loaded a bus and drove to the courthouse. I shake my head as I'm exiting the bus. It almost feels like deja vu. The last time I was here, six people were shot and killed, and the judge ended up in intensive care. They canceled court of course and postponed everyone's court dates. Walking into the court being directed back to the jury box, I remember the events as though they happened yesterday. I tell you what, though, they are beyond prepared this time. There are two guards at the door we entered, two at the door the spectators, lawyers and citizens enter, and two at each end of where the judge sits. A person would be an idiot to try something with all these officers in here now. The poor judge probably is still scared for her life. I know somebody else who needs to be scared for their life too. Revenge is a motherfucker.

I see Peter and my lawyers enter as well as the minute clerk, law clerk, and court reporter. The district attorney enters nervously again, looking at the jury box, never making eye contact. People commence piling in, so I'm sure court is getting ready to start. Where the hell is Janae? She promised she would be here. I need her support. Hell, I need her strength. My lawyers both walk and sit at the defense desk. They look at me and nod. Oh my God! I must be up first! My body begins to tingle, and I immediately get hot. I begin to sweat nervously, while my eyes scan the courtroom. Where is Janae?! Ugh!

I hope Judge Francis is in a good mood and the previous events of being back in this courtroom don't have a bad effect on her!

The bailiff comes out saying, "All rise! Thirty-Third Criminal District Court is now in session. The honorable Judge Charlotte E. Francis presiding."

"Good morning, ladies and gentlemen. Please turn your attention to the left corner where our American flag is. Please place your right hand over your heart and recite with me the pledge of allegiance," says Judge Francis.

"You may now be seated," says the bailiff.

A couple of stragglers come in the courtroom, quietly taking a seat in the back but none of them are Janae. This is not like her. She's late every once in a while, but never for anything important such as this. She needs to hurry! I begin to remember our last conversation about Evon. What if he's done something to her? She was supposed to be trying to find him to find out what the hell is going on. Where he came from, how long has he been here, and did he kill Dev? Deep down, I don't think it was Dev hurt Janae I think it was Evon, and the more I think about it the scarier the situation is because she may have played right into his hands. I wonder if Peter has talked to her? I notice he keeps looking around. I wonder if he's looking for her? My God, my God! Please wrap your arms around her and keep her safe! I scream inwardly with a tear swelling in my right eye.

This time, Judge Francis doesn't have a laptop in front of her. She already has a pen in hand and has business written all over her face.

"Calling the case of the people of Louisiana vs Jazmynn Olivia Barkley. Are both sides ready?" asks Judge Francis in a scruffy voice.

I wonder if her voice has something to do with her getting shot. Poor lady. She seems nice enough. She really didn't deserve that!

The district attorney stands and says, "Yes, your honor, if it pleases the court, my name is Authur Bushwell and I appear for the prosecution."

My lawyers then stand, the handsome one going first saying. "Yes, your honor, if it pleases the court, my name is David Arceneaux and I appear for the defense," the other lawyer says. "Yes, your honor, if it pleases the court, my name is Benjamin Edwards and I also appear for the defense."

Judge Francis says, "Thank you, counsel. Please read the charges to the accused."

One of the guards stands and walks me over to the desk my lawyers sit to. I stand there in my shackles, unsure of what to do. So I just stand staring at Judge Francis.

"We are here today with case number 12-1-00858-5," says one of the ladies sitting by the judge. Jazmynn Olivia Barkley, you have been charged under section 13A of the Criminal Law Consolidation Act 2012 of first-degree murder of Devon Edward Thomas and the attempted murder of Janae Christian Carter. How do you plead?"

How do I plead? What? What do you think? "NOT GUILTY," I respond confidently.

Hell, what did they expect? I've been locked up all this time and I'm now going to change my plea?! It still the same! I didn't fucking kill Devon and I most definitely won't take the charge for it, plus they can dismiss the attempted murder on Janae. Her testimony will prove it wasn't me who shot her; it was indeed Dev or Evon's trifling ass!

About the Author

Lorenza Fontenot is a thirty-three-year-old branch manager and interlibrary loan specialist at the Allen Parish Libraries in Oberlin, La. She resides in Oberlin, La, with her husband, black lab named Ace, and her chinchilla named Kenzi. *Scandalous Jazmynn* is her first published work that she hopes will become a bestseller. When she is not at work, or working on her book, she enjoys writing poetry. She hopes to continue *Scandalous Jazmynn* into a series.

CPSIA information can be obtained
at www.ICGtesting.com
Printed in the USA
LVHW010824300321
682936LV00010B/180